LOVE CHANGES

Written By: Carrie B. Farley

Love Changes

Copyright © 2020 by Beauty From Ashes, LLC

ISBN: 978-1-716-33047-6

Dedication & Acknowledgements

I would like to thank God for the writing ability and for allowing me to continually grow in this area. I pray as I continue to write more books, that they are for Your glory.

My mother, Frances Marr… **"Wind Beneath My Wings,"** we got through another one, again! I love you forever.

My husband, Jermaine…Thanks for your critiques and suggestions…you along with Jordynn and Calynn for the **sacrifices** of family time that were made while writing this book. Your **support** means more to me than anything.

To my **"Pretty Girls Club"**: Jashayla Jennings, Lei'Ana Rodriguez, and Mi'Ana Berry…thanks for the plot ideas surrounding the teenage characters. I love you to life!

To my cousin April-Christina aka **"Stina Bina"** and my girl, Gloria Mallory aka **"Glow"**…thank you guys for sitting through me reading the story at times to you guys as a sounding board. I thank you, thank you, thank you!

Special Thanks: Moneeka Gentry-Stanifer of CreatedbyMoneeka for the dope cover design…you rock! Trotwood fam is always gonna be fam!

***This book is dedicated to those who have survived this monumental time of the COVID-19 pandemic. May we all stay covered and protected as we navigate through life's journey to finding and operating in our purpose and callings in their respective places…life is way too short!

***This "Love Series" will ALWAYS be dedicated to my father, the late Boyde L. Marr…Forever a **"Daddy's Girl."**

Hangover

"Mommy, can I go over to Londyn's for the weekend so I can go to Smyrna with her and her mom? Garb has a huge sale…" asked Tania, Ondrea's mocha-colored and deep dimpled, sixteen-year-old daughter with a former lover, Chance. The two had just returned to their home in North Buckhead from grabbing lunch together at Slutty Vegan.

"Sure, if they're going to pick you up and bring you back home."

Ondrea hung up the keys to her 2021 Infiniti QX50 and plopped down on the sofa in the living room to watch some HGTV.

"Thanks, Mommy…you're the best!" she squealed hugging her mom with excitement, before releasing her grip to dial Londyn's phone number on her cell phone.

As Ondrea saw it, it was not hard to oblige anything that her daughter asked of her due to the damaging reality that she had to grow up just like her—never a *"daddy's girl."*

Nevertheless, Tania Paige Williams had been her anchor during the fifteen years that Ondrea has spent in mourning. Chance Williams—the love of her life—was murdered execution-style here in Atlanta, Georgia. There was not a single day that went by in which those memories of how they were and what they used to do consumed Ondrea's mind. Upon graduating from Spelman College, and more recently becoming a Forensic Psychologist, Ondrea understood that in the realm of grief and loss, severe grief for this long has not been healthy mentally for her.

Ondrea's Aunt Shelby and Bria, her best friend would constantly remind her of how important it was for her to "let Chance go." The truth of the matter was that although no one would ever be able to replace the void of Tania's father, Ondrea also knew that in her decision to not allow someone else to again have her heart, was also robbing her daughter of the potential fulfillment that comes with being able to experience a father's love while growing up—while being able to see an example of how a man should treat her.

Some men have previously tried to entertain her company, but to no avail, they just did not and could not measure up to Chance. She just cannot seem to let go.

<u>Chapter One</u>

It had been almost four months since she had last seen Bria, her husband Dearron and nine-month-old, Jonoah Matthew--their new addition, and Ondrea's godson. After Bria and Dearron married in 2001, they packed up and moved to Savannah, Georgia, where he went to help take care of his terminally ill grandmother while cutting hair on the side. Only a year later, he accepted the call to preach the gospel of Jesus Christ, while Bria finished her Accounting degree at Georgia State University. Earlier this year, Dearron become one of the most respected and well-known pastors in Savannah, and Bria became one of KRT CPA's "Most Valuable Players." Just before the birth of their son, they were able to purchase a home located in the beautiful Coffee Pointe subdivision.

Over the years, Bria longed deeply for Ondrea's healing of her broken heart and would never stop to go as far as trying to convince Ondrea to leave the townhome that Chance had purchased for them before his death and move closer to her for strength as well as a new beginning for her and Tania. Although Ondrea stated time and time again that she did not want to "go to church like that," Bria still invited her to any and every program that they had had. Bria had invited Ondrea for the weekend to help her celebrate Dearron's 5th Pastoral Anniversary and was ecstatic this time around that Ondrea took her up on one of her invites.

"I might as well go since Tania's leaving me this weekend, I can see my godson, and I did forget I RSVP'd to their church event last month back in June…Bria would be so mad at me if I flaked on her…" Ondrea reasoned with herself.

*****

Not long after Londyn's mother picked Tania up, Ondrea was back in her SUV, with her bag packed and jamming to some Brandy bracing herself for the 3 ½ hour-long drive she had to Savannah, Georgia. She had her playlist ready: Cardi B, Joe, Tank, Inayah Lamis, Carl Thomas, Monica, and Meg Thee Stallion to name a few.

Upon pulling into the beautifully gated community, Ondrea began to briefly consider the thought of moving somewhere closer, but immediately snapped back out of it… *"that will never happen… I have no problems visiting them anytime they ask, however going to church all the time is just something I cannot see myself doing…and my condominium is bought and paid for…Who would want to go back to a mortgage?"* she questioned herself.

"Hey, cow!" Bria exclaimed once she opened the double front doors to their lovely home with one arm, and Jonoah in the other. She and Ondrea had adopted the term *"cow"* after the two best friends in their favorite movie Poetic Justice.

"Hey, cow!" Ondrea responded, laying her luggage down to hug both Bria and Jonoah.

"Let me put him down so we can chit-chat," squealed Bria.

Ondrea sat down on one of the couches in the living room and waited for Bria to return. Being a pastor's wife is a very lonely position; oftentimes one in which Bria stated that she hardly had anyone to talk to but another friend of hers named Taylor who also is the First Lady. Until she met Taylor, Bria's transition was a difficult one. In their earlier days, between the two of them; Bria was always considered the "wild one." Bria testifies that if it was not for Taylor's guidance along with the patience of Dearron and the congregation, Dearron may have found himself without her by his side in ministry—let alone the two of them still even married. From the results of Taylor's interventions, Bria's tearful late-night vent sessions started to decrease with time, and in turn, the congregation began to fully welcome her as a part of her husband's ministry.

7

"So, how's everything going 'Drea?" Bria asked emerging back from Jonoah's room, "how's my 'Taniecy-pooh?'"

Ondrea sighed, "Girl, she is already bugging me about this "Sweet 16" skating party that she planned. From talking about how she wants Luke James to sing 'Happy Birthday' to her, to the entire freshman class that she wants to invite, all the way down to the already-parked-outside, S 560 Mercedes-Benz coupe at the skating rink that she hopes everyone will go on Facebook live to show off...I mean, she is doing the entire most!"

"Oh, my goodness, what is she going to want for her graduation then?! Are you thinking about doing all of that for her?! What are her grades looking like?"

"She made National Honor Society again, Straight A's all four quarters, and they voted her President of the Spanish club for next school year…"

"...Well, then you have to show up and out for her then, 'Mommie Dearest'!" Bria playfully responded, throwing one of her couch pillows at Ondrea.

"As if!" she exclaimed throwing the pillow back at Bria while laughing, "I'm not going to be on anyone's payment plans with all kinds of debt...tell you what, I'm going to let you and 'D fund the entire shindig, sissy...just wait until 'Noah gets Tania's age...I can't wait to tease you about all the little girls that'll be calling the house."

"How many boys call Tania now?"

"For now, I believe it's just the one… The boy's name is Sebastian that she's been hanging with him more frequently...Lord knows I can't deal with any other ones sniffing around...with Tyrin and his crew always watching her, there shouldn't be any drama when it comes to Tania. If so, you know he will get involved."

8

Tyrin has been a huge help to Ondrea and Tania wherever he sees a need. After Chance's murder, he made sure that in addition to Ondrea's cousin Marie, Aunt Shelby, Bria, and Dearron, that she knew they had family on Chance's side that could be counted on.

"How's he doing, by-the-way?" Bria asked as her body posture changed from relaxed to a more intense fixture while sitting on the couch, "Wasn't he locked up for three years or something?"

"Yes, it was three...he's doing alright...he has his car detailing shop, along with some investments he began after Chance died... I'll tell him you asked about him."

"I just asked that's all...no need to relay any messages," she replied in an awkward response.

Ondrea knew that Bria and Tyrin had hooked up at some point during their senior year in high school. The fact that he was the most popular junior-to-be, Quarterback of the Varsity football team, in addition to the next-in-line to inherit Chance's financial success that he had made before getting out of *"the life,"* had always excited her. Dearron never knew this occurred, and Ondrea vowed that she would keep their secret to Bria—even though Bria will probably never admit to it. Acknowledging the uncomfortable tone in her response, Ondrea quickly switched subjects.

"So how are you and Dearron doing?" I know you guys better be careful with your first year after giving birth because you're very fertile during this time."

"Girl, I probably won't be able to carry any more babies due to the excessive scarring from all those abortions I had back in the day...I thank God I was able to have the one for him... 'D' is good, the congregation being so needy all the time is what I wish could calm down some."

"If your hubby wasn't at that TD Jakes status right now, then maybe the demand wouldn't be so bad," Ondrea joked. "Again, I love your home, sissy."

"Oh, I forgot to give you a tour," Bria stated as she got up from the couch, "lemme hurry up and do it before 'D' comes back with his preacher friend...I want to show you the whole house."

"What preacher friend?" Ondrea inquired.

Bria perked up, "You're inquiring about somebody now?!"

"No, I'm just being nosey on who he's bringing to you guys' house that's all. You know how protective Dearron is about his private life...he must be good peoples."

"Well, his name is Kamal Davis. He is supposed to be the next big preacher out of Marietta, and he's 'D's guest speaker on tonight...they met at some prayer breakfast a few months back, 'D' liked his spirit...also, the word on the street is the only reason he isn't a pastor yet, is because he's single..."

"...Bria, stop!" Ondrea interjected, "I am not in the mood for your hookups."

"Don't flatter yourself, the world doesn't revolve around you 'dearie'," Bria said with a smirk, "however if you change your mind..."

Just then, Bria got a call from Dearron on her cell phone stating that he and Minister Kamal were running behind schedule and that he would have to just meet up with her at the church.

After Bria finished giving Ondrea the tour, she then showed her the guest room in which she would be sleeping in. After Bria left, Ondrea immediately unzipped her Louis Vuitton luggage and spread her clothes out to see what she could wear tonight for the service. By the time it was time to go, she was cute and conservative in a blue Balenciaga suit. For some reason, she started getting a little anxious. "*Just who this mystery man is that suddenly 'D is cool with? Oh, chill out, 'Drea,*" she told herself, "*this isn't even how you operate... 'Team Chance' ALWAYS!*"

Chapter Two

"Oh, He kept me/ God kept me/ He kept me, so I wouldn't let go…" were the melodious words

sang by the choir that night. Ondrea sang right along with them. She loved her some Kurt Carr, and you could

catch her singing songs from the <u>Awesome Wonder</u> cd any day. She looked down at her Apple watch, and no

sooner as she looked back up, in walked with Dearron a man who had the smoothest dark-chocolate skin tone,

chiseled features who strongly favored the realtor—turned model, Donnel Blaylock. Ondrea tried not to focus

too hard on his appearance; however, she found her eyes could not break away from him as he walked into the

sanctuary, and across the pulpit. His presence just commanded the attention of everyone that was in the room.

After Dearron introduced Minister Kamal Davis to the congregation and visitors, he spoke, and the deep

baritone in his voice made it even that much harder for Ondrea to keep her attention on the Word of God. She

stared upfront in the direction of Bria, trying to catch her attention while she was sitting in her chair designated

for the First Lady, but at that point in the service, Bria's attention was given to her husband while he continued

his remarks on Minister Davis.

Minister Davis then shook Dearron's hand and opened his Bible as he prepared to address the people.

"Please open up your Bibles, as well as your hearts to receive 1 Peter 5:7 and 2 Corinthians 10:4," he

stated. "...and it reads 'Casting all your care upon him; for He careth for you'...and 'For out of much affliction

and anguish of heart I wrote unto you with many tears; not that ye should be grieved, but that ye might know

the love which I have more'...my thought on tonight comes from 1 Peter 5:7...'Cast It Down.'"

He then began to expound on the thought of being able to relinquish our fears, as well as all things that

were troubling us to the Lord. As he continued to minister, Ondrea could not help but to tear up from the

11

anxious feeling deep down on the inside of her. Nervous to explore those feelings, Ondrea reached into her matching Balenciaga clutch to retrieve her iPhone, checking to see if Tania tried to call or text her.

In his closing remarks, Minister Davis then asked if anyone wanted to give their lives to Christ, or if they were backslidden, and/or needed to be filled or re-filled with the Holy Spirit. A couple of people stood up and came forward. Minister Davis prayed with power for those who received salvation, and the demonstration of the Holy Ghost filled the room as the Spirit gave utterance in two of the souls who came to Christ.

During the altar call, Ondrea felt a strong sense that he was looking in her direction, and as soon as she looked up from her phone, Minister Davis pointed at her, "Excuse me, the lady in the blue, can I pray for you?"

Not wanting to make a scene, she nodded her head yes, and made her way to the front of the church. The palms of her hands began to sweat profusely with each step taken towards the altar.

Minister Davis took his hand into hers, "What's your name?"

While normally the overwhelming feeling of being put on the spot would have occurred, his touch felt comforting.

"Ondrea," she replied.

"Ondrea, I don't know you, but the Lord does, and He wants you to know that He has always loved and looked out for you."

Ondrea instantly felt the back of her neck start to heat up with anger. *The Lord can't possibly love me because if He did, He wouldn't have the love of my life and father of my child be murdered and taken out of our lives just like he allowed my parents to be taken from me!"*

Immediately, the tears started to well up in her eyes, and she began to shake her head no in disbelief.

12

Minister Davis looked into Ondrea's eyes with an intense stare and she turned away. He then squeezed her hands gently with reassurance and continued, "God says that He sees your tears and has heard your cries, and that void you've constantly been trying to fill will only be fulfilled through gaining a closer relationship with Him. You may not believe, nor choose to receive what I am saying to you...however I'm just the messenger...do you receive the Word from the Lord on tonight, Ondrea?"

"Y...y...yes," she stammered as the tears began to stream down her face. As he let go of her hands and placed his hand on top of her head to pray over her, she let out a loud, sharp, and piercing scream—and then suddenly she felt something that she had never felt in fifteen years...peace.

Chapter Three

"So, how'd you enjoy the service?" Bria asked.

Ondrea was still in awe of her experience on the altar with Minister Davis, "It was okay…very different than any other service I've ever attended before…I felt something on that altar that I haven't felt, and that's peace of mind."

"Well, I'm happy for you sissy!" she exclaimed, "Do you think it was because you received the Holy Spirit as a comforter?"

"I'm not sure yet, I just know for right now I feel good."

"So…. what do you think about Minister Davis…"

"…I knew you were gonna try and go there," Ondrea interjected, "don't start that…"

"Girl, ain't he a fine piece of chocolate Heaven though?" Bria asked.

"Yes, he is, but…"

"…No buts, 'Drea!" Bria interrupted for a second time, "That man is single, anointed, and fine…you better act like you know, okay?!"

Bria then went upstairs to put Jonoah down in his crib, leaving Ondrea in the kitchen to start punching in a pizza order online from their Samsung refrigerator, when the garage door began to open.

"Hey 'D'," Ondrea called out nonchalantly, "that was a great service on tonight."

"Well praise the Lord, 'lady in the blue', He gets all the glory," called out the familiar deep voice that held her hands and prayed the prayer of release over Ondrea's life.

Startled, she jumped a little, "Oh, Minister Davis, I wasn't aware that you'd be coming back here with Dearron…"

Dearron entered the house ahead of Minister Davis following up playfully, "Yeah, I wanted to show him around and catch up earlier before the service, but we didn't have time…is that okay with you, 'Drea?"

"Oh, I didn't mean it like that, 'D…" Ondrea hurried to explain, "…Bria just went upstairs a little while ago to put 'Noah down…excuse me, gentlemen," she stated and made every effort to quickly leave out of their presence. *Why couldn't I look Minister Davis in his eyes? I am tripping,* she thought to herself.

Ondrea hurried up the stairs and as soon as her feet touched the top of the second-floor stairwell, she whispered for Bria to step into the hallway out from Jonoah's room and motioned for Bria to follow her into the guest bedroom.

"Girl, you didn't tell me that 'D was bringing Minister Davis home with him after the service!"

"I know right?! So fun to keep secrets from you…girl, 'D invited him; I told you they got super cool when they met at that prayer breakfast." Bria replied. "We can just put our pajamas and scarves on, go downstairs, and just chill and watch movies in the living room—eating our pizza when it comes—we won't even be in the same room as them."

"I guess…gimme a sec and I'll meet you downstairs," she replied hesitantly.

Before heading downstairs to join Bria, Ondrea made sure that her hair was brushed back into a ponytail, and that she was comfortable in her midnight blue Victoria's Secret PINK pajama set with the matching house shoes. Just as she began to head downstairs, the doorbell rings.

"I got it, babe!" exclaimed Dearron as he headed towards the door to retrieve the pizza, "Kamal, you can just go in the living room with Bria and 'Drea, and I'll bring the food in there."

Bria and Ondrea both looked at each other in surprise, as they both knew that this night was going to get interesting, to say the least. Ondrea's eyes then wandered to the doorway, as Minister Davis entered the room. She noticed that he was wearing a black Tom Ford suit, with yellow as his accent color. They briefly locked eyes, and she immediately looked away. Minister Davis chuckled to himself at her response.

"You and Dearron have a beautiful home...love the artwork, it has to be Detroit's own... Lock Art, right?" he stated to Bria as he looked around, gazing at the commissioned pieces hanging designed by the infamous Jamar Lockhart from Detroit, Michigan. His artwork was world-wide renown, and the hottest commodity on the artistic scene as of lately.

"Why thank you, Minister Davis," she stated, grinning proudly.

"Please, you guys can just call me Kamal, when I'm not preaching," he stated.

"I understand that however you still represent Christ regardless of wherever you may be," Ondrea replied.

"True, true...however, we are all called to represent Him at all times, therefore, I'm no different from you..." he responded.

"...Y'all better back up off my man's, tryna tag-team a brotha of the cloth!" Dearron playfully interjected while bringing in the food with paper plates on top of the box.

"Whatever," stated Bria, as she got up from the couch, "Ondrea, come on and let's get some drinks out the kitchen," she retorted.

As Ondrea got up from the loveseat sofa and walked out of the room, she felt Minister Davis' eyes watching. *This is too intense*, she thought to herself...*Team Chance, 'Drea...*

Once the ladies joined Dearron and Minister Kamal back in the living room, the guys had turned from the Urban Movie Network's Season 2 <u>Monogamy</u> series they started, to Netflix's Season 1 of the <u>Marlon</u> show.

"Well, thanks a lot...You better be glad your show is good too!" exclaimed Bria, as she started to plop down next to Dearron on the couch.

"You're welcome, babe," he replied playfully as he gave her a quick smack on her butt.

"Alright, you two," Ondrea replied in her best "Mother Dearest" voice and pointed up at the stairs, "that's exactly how you guys got my godson..."

"...Don't hate on them," replied Minister Davis, "just because your man isn't here sitting next to you doesn't mean you gotta take it out on them," he jokingly added.

Ondrea then gave him one of her best dirty looks.

"Touchy subject, huh?" he laughed as he bit his bottom lip.

Ondrea turned to look away from him again, as his look was so intense and the image of him biting his lip was starting to excite her. Bria and Dearron were now looking in her direction in anticipation—wondering how she was going to respond to Minister Davis' comment.

"It's complicated..." she replied, getting up from the loveseat. "Goodnight Minister Davis, 'D... Bria..." As the tears started to form, Ondrea quickly left the room careful not to break down and cry in front of everyone. *Why was I so emotional?!* She thought angrily to herself. *Why did I let a simple joke bother me the way that it did? 'Drea. get it together!*

*****

Bria and Dearron apologized to Minister Davis in assuming that introducing them would have been a good idea at this time and that Ondrea had been through a lot and normally would not have responded to him the way that she did. Bria then excused herself to check on Ondrea.

"'Drea, what was that all about," Bria asked while knocking on the bedroom door. By now, Ondrea was laying in the bed underneath the sheet with all the covers pulled up over her head. She had felt so embarrassed, upset, and scared…*scared of what though?*

"I don't know, Bria! I just got so overwhelmed with what he said to me because it was partly true. I haven't been 'happy-in-love' since Chance, and the fact that he called that out on tonight just took me aback some," she admitted.

Bria immediately reached out to hug her, "Sissy, I am so sorry, and trust if I knew that, I wouldn't be trying to throw it in your face…"

"…I'm not saying that" Ondrea interjected, "I'm just saying through his interactions, he made me aware of some things that I have yet and need to deal with…he probably thinks I'm this evil-crazy lady now?" she lamented while lifting a Kleenex tissue from the box on the nightstand and drying her face.

"So, you do care how he perceives you, huh?" asked Bria.

"First impressions are lasting ones, you know?" she replied jokingly.

A big smile began to spread across Bria's face, "Yay, I was hoping there'd be something there between the two of you…"

"...No, Bria…I'm not saying it as I like him like that or anything…"

"…Okay, 'Drea," Bria sarcastically responded, "I'm sure even Stevie Wonder can see and know that man is fine," she added as she closed back the bedroom door and went back down the hall to check on Jonoah.

*****

After about half an hour had passed, there was a knock on the bedroom door.

"Bria, I'm good now…I promise," Ondrea stated.

"Sorry to disappoint you, but it's Kamal," the voice answered back.

"What are you doing up here, Minister Davis?" she asked through the door—careful not to open it.

"I want to apologize if I offended you. That was definitely not my intent, and I was hoping you wouldn't mind me making it up to you by taking you out tomorrow while you're here in town, and before I head back home."

Boy, did his line seem all too familiar… "Well, that's very nice of you, and I accept your apology, however, we're not together for you to call yourself taking me out anywhere to 'makeup'," Ondrea added flirtatiously.

"Baby steps, 'lady-in-the-blue'," he smoothly replied, "I have to admit, I am intrigued by the thought of getting to know the beautiful woman behind this door."

"Thanks, but I'm leaving to head back home tomorrow morning," Ondrea stated, wanting to open the door, but not knowing after looking into his eyes what other feelings could be invoked. She kept it closed, "but I'll take a rain check."

"Where do you live, if you don't mind me asking?"

19

"I stay in North Buckhead."

"Dang, so you're like fifteen minutes away from me then…" he said matter-of-factly, "before I get ahead of myself, and go into putting all this effort into getting to know you, are you engaged or in a serious relationship?"

"I told you it's complicated."

"Then how about we have more conversation about that situation?"

"Okay, Minister Davis," she then replied respectively, "make sure you get my number from 'D'," she further added.

"I'll do that," he replied cool and calmly to himself as he slowly walked away from the bedroom door where she was sleeping.

Kamal was eagerly excited to get to learn more about Ondrea, but reminded himself that all things may be lawful, but not expedient and therefore he did not want to rush to his judgment or feelings, and more importantly—the timing. He had to be sure about what the connection was to be with this mysterious new woman whom he had the pleasure of having the encounter while praying for her on the altar on tonight. Kamal knew that for him to keep his focus and grow even further into ultimately a successful pastor like his friend Dearron, he needed to be married. He for sure did not want to confuse a possibly great friendship with Ondrea versus her being wife potential. He needed someone by his side to be able to pray him through all the trials and tribulations that he would be faced within all the territory that comes with new levels that bring about new devils. He had been pulled out of Hell once and had no plans of returning to that life ever again.

Chapter Four

As she glanced at her dark-brown complexion and applied her Brittney Kelley Brands "Carrie" shade of lipstick, Ondrea could not help but replay her exchange of words in her conversation with Kamal. She had to admit that there was some curiosity there in seeing what he was all about, and how God could use him to help her to feel what she so longed and desired for years. *Was it meant for just that moment, or was there something more?*

She snapped out of her daze and headed downstairs making sure that all her bags were packed and by the front door for Dearron to help take to her car. As Ondrea said her goodbyes to Dearron, Bria motioned for Ondrea to come with her into the kitchen as she grabbed Jonoah's bottle. She hugged and kissed Jonoah, passing him back to Dearron, and braced herself for the infamous grilling she was going to receive from Bria.

"Girl! What happened between the two of you last night because that man was sweating 'D' for your number when he came back downstairs?!"

"Nothing happened, Bria. He just apologized for offending me and tried to see if I would let him take me out…"

"So, my question is why are you leaving right now, then? He's not leaving town until morning service on Sunday," Bria interjected.

"Number one: I need to make sure I'm home and settled before Tania gets back, and number two: I don't want to seem so available and desperate…"

"Cow, you ARE available, and CAN be desperate for him…"

"Then why don't you divorce 'D' and be with him, as much as you are geeking over him…" Ondrea interrupted.

"Okay, you have officially lost your mind, 'Drea. I am married, but I am also not blind. I am talking about him being strictly matched for you, boo! Again, if he is trying to take you out and treat you good, he already helped assist you in getting some of your joy back, give him a chance."

"I recall you telling me to give Chance a 'chance,' and look at what happened to us…."

"You totally cannot compare the two…two totally different men. That is what exercising your faith is, 'Drea…"

"I have none," Ondrea retorted back as she headed out of their kitchen and down the hallway towards the front door to exit.

Bria grabbed her arm and turned Ondrea back around to face her, "Ondrea, I am praying for you and believing in God that you find some—even if it's the size of a mustard seed…again, I will repeat myself…do not waste your life away by letting fear paralyze you, sissy. You deserve the good life that God has in store for you!"

With tears starting to form again, Ondrea hugged her best friend of over 20+ years, "thank you for the hospitality, and I love you." She then turned back around to leave out of Bria and Dearron's house to start her drive back home.

Chapter Five

Ondrea felt her eyes starting to get heavy while driving. *Another hour and a half... I can make it!* Just then, her cell phone began to ring.

"RING!!!"

She casually answered via Bluetooth, "Hello, talk to me."

"I'm going to tell you right now that I only want to speak to Ms. Lady-in-the-Blue," that deep voice firmly stated back.

Suddenly, Ondrea felt that burst of energy she needed to get to her destination.

"That 'lady-in-the-blue's' name is Ondrea Robertson," she playfully replied, "and yes she is available to talk at the moment."

"Well, woman put her on the phone!" he jokingly exclaimed.

"Why, hello...may I ask who is calling for me?"

"Thirty-nine-year-old, Kamal Davis from Marietta, Georgia. I am single—and looking...however, I'm just going to cut to the chase...currently, I am trying to get to know more of and about you."

Ondrea was taken aback by Kamal's forwardness. It was also quite the turn-on as well, as this was one of the things she had missed in her dealings with Chance.

"Well, Mr. Davis...I am thirty-three years old, and from Atlanta, Georgia. I am single; however, I am not sure if I want to be found or take any applications right now..."

"May I ask why?" he interrupted with a tone now more serious and direct, "I mean, what's the issue? Do you have a lot of kids? Crazy baby-daddy? What's up?"

"Well," he heard Ondrea's voice crack, "I have one daughter who will be sixteen soon, and her father, unfortunately, is not a part of mine or his daughter's anymore."

"Okay," he began to soften his tone and relaxed more, "I'm sorry to hear that he is absent from you guys' lives...I don't want to pressure you to disclose more than you are ready to share. As I told you last night, I know there is a connection between us, and that is not like me to ever have that kind of connection with any random woman on the altar, at the church where I am an Associate Pastor—ANY woman for that matter. I owe it to myself to find out what kind of connection this TRULY may be. I can't lie—I'd be remiss if I did hesitate on letting you know how I felt...you know you're an extremely beautiful woman."

Ondrea felt herself blush. "Well, Mr. Davis I deeply appreciate you not wanting to waste my time, and I don't want to waste yours. I have to admit that you also are quite easy on the eyes..."

"I can't tell—you wouldn't even open the door to look at my face last night..." he playfully interjected, "...make me feel like I have the 'cooties' or something."

Ondrea let out a hearty laugh—something a man had not been able to achieve with her—*No! Team Chance, 'Drea!!!* "Maybe you do. I do not know you like that...what about you... Kids? Crazy ex...baby-mama drama?"

"Nope, nope, and nope to all of your answers.

"I find that extremely hard to believe. As clean-cut as you are, women probably throw themselves at you...I am not buying that...no kids? Yeah right."

"There's a lot more to me than what people perceive. I have had my share of women, but that was from another time from another life. I give God all the glory and honor from where He has brought me from, and with no children from all that mess I was in. With serious consecration by prayer and fasting, I am a lot more self-disciplined now, and I'm able to restrain myself from my fleshly desires."

"So, then you must be one of those men who continually pray?" Ondrea asked jokingly.

"I have to," he stated matter-of-factly, "if not I'd be most miserable and without the power that God gives me when I get up to speak before His people."

"I see," Ondrea replied, finally turning off from the highway and then proceeding to let him know she was now about twenty minutes from home.

"You didn't say whether or not you felt any kind of connection or chemistry? I'm curious to know your thoughts…" he quickly added back into their conversation simultaneously as Ondrea was trying to wrap it up.

Team Chance… She did not want to be honest with him… "There is something there," she hesitantly admitted. Ondrea felt convicted as she knew she could not lie—especially to a preacher—*why was it so easy to talk with him? He made me laugh…*she thought to herself.

"Is that 'something' worth exploring to you?"

"Part of me is saying yes, and the other is saying to just leave things be the way that they are…"

"Well, we're just going to have to see where this thing goes to find out what perception is the right one. Ms. Robertson, are you available to join me for Sunday service?"

"You mean turn around and drive back to Savannah right now, and then have to drive back again tomorrow evening?!"

26

"You're right," he said realizing the distance, "I'll have to figure something out… in the meantime, I really would like for you to see the church that I preach in—I mean, I ain't trying to be your pastor or nothing, but I am wondering what you'd think about dating a preacher or pastor, should we find out this connection is more than just a spiritual one."

"We can cross that road if we get there…right now, I'm not that strong in my faith to be anyone's anchor, First lady—none of that at all."

"Well, again time will tell everything, and something tells me that you are stronger than you think…have you made it home safely yet?" he asked with concern.

"Turning in my driveway now, daddy," she playfully retorted.

"And my praying starts back up… right about now," he chuckled, but also serious as he shifted into an upright position in the bed at the hotel where he was staying for the weekend. *She cannot play with me like that while I am laying here,* he lamented to himself. *Lord, I need for her to be the one because I cannot keep these urges suppressed around her for long—I can tell,* he prayed silently to himself.

From his response, Ondrea knew that she had said something that was a turn on and immediately apologized to him for possibly introducing an inappropriate thought in his head. *You can't play that way with a man of God, 'Drea,* she told herself.

"Thanks for being thoughtful; however, my mind is what took your comment out of the context you meant. That is something that I must stay cognizant about. As I stated before, you are an incredibly beautiful woman. Whenever I am entertaining you—whether it is via phone or in person, I know now for sure I better be prayed up."

"I appreciate your honesty…there's that chemistry revealing itself you were talking about, I presume?"

"Indeed, Ms. Robertson," he replied coolly.

Ondrea could feel herself wanting to get more engaged in exploring his wild side during this conversation, but she decided that she would not tempt the man of God any more than she already had.

"How about on Mondays, we make that our day to talk and see how our week was," he proposed.

"Mondays are fine. I can get my weekly words of encouragement and wisdom from you…"

"What you mean?" he asked in a serious tone again. "Do you not have a pastor that you can listen to and get fed the Word? You know faith comes by hearing and hearing…"

"I honestly haven't been to a church in years. Yesterday was the first time that I walked into a church service since I had stopped going…yeah, um it is complicated…I am a work in progress, so let's appreciate the baby steps."

"…As we all are…alright, I'll talk to you on Monday then, Ondrea."

"Alright, Minister Davis."

She pulled into her driveway, turned the ignition off, breathed in deeply and slowly, and exhaled. Truthfully, Ondrea did not know if she could wait until Monday to speak with him. She was falling fast, *but so was he, wasn't he?* She knew she could not afford to go back down the path of falling for someone quick without taking things slow before going all in. *Reel it back in, 'Drea.*

Chapter Six

Once inside and after resting some, the motion detector alerted Ondrea that someone was in the driveway. She then peeked through the blinds, and it was Tania getting ready to get out of Grace Turner's Tesla.

Londyn's mother, Grace was retired from the military, and Mr. Turner was a prominent neurosurgeon in the local area hospital close to home. They were ecstatic to know that their daughter had found a new friend who had *"morals"* and her *"head on straight,"* as Grace stated to Ondrea, assuring that they would treat Tania as if she were their own whenever she was in their company. After learning that Tania's father was deceased as time went on, they became huge blessings to both Ondrea and Tania.

Ondrea eyed the Neiman Marcus and Garb shopping bags she had carried in the house in addition to her overnight bag.

"So, how was Smyrna?"

"It was lit! Londynn's mom bought me and her matching Gucci belt bags and matching blue jean rompers…we just have to get through August, and then we're gonna showcase our outfits on 'em at the homecoming game and party."

"You are so spoiled," Ondrea replied.

"Nope, just loved," Tania jokingly replied, "how was your weekend, Mom?"

"It was alright. I decided to go to Savannah and spend some time with your Aunt Bria, Uncle D, and 'Noah…"

"…Really, Mom!" she pouted, "You know I wanted to see them too!"

"Calm down, I'll probably head back down that way sometime soon…you can come with me on the next trip…the baby is so cute by the way…"

"I don't even want to hear anymore because you're rubbing it in…bye Felicia," Tania retorted as she put up her "girl bye" hand and stormed out of the living room. *Teenagers.*

About five minutes later, Ondrea gets an incoming call from Bria. "Hey, cow! Have you made it home, yet?"

"Oh, I'm sorry that I didn't let you know, girl…I totally forgot."

"Mmm-hmmm …so, how did that happen? Someone else occupies my phone time?" Bria pried.

"Actually, 'D's' friend called me, and we ended up talking until I got home."

"Really?!" exclaimed Bria jumping up and down, almost forgetting she was holding Jonoah, "I am so glad to hear that…so, how was the conversation?"

"He definitely has a wild side—you can tell—but he actually kept it very respectful and even tried to get me to tell him more about my situation. He asked me to come to his church sometime, and we kind of agreed to talk once a week just to start to get to know each other. He said that he felt we had a connection, I told him I just don't know if I'm ready for any kind of relationship right now at this point."

"That's fair, however, that man is interested in you, girl…no baggage, no previous marriages or divorces…no kids from what 'D' has told me…"

"Yeah, I know. But it is too good to be true. Bria, I don't want to get hurt again…you know my heart can't take anymore."

30

"God doesn't put any more on you than you can bear...remember that, always. He's seen you through to grow up without your natural parents, brought you through the trauma surrounding Chance with having to raise Tania as a single mom, and He will continue to see you through the rest of your journey...God has so much in store for you, sissy."

"Speaking of Tania, she is very upset with me that I didn't bring her when I came," Ondrea quickly changed the subject, "I told her that I will bring her the next time I come."

"Well, good cow," Bria said annoyingly, "back to the subject at hand—you need to stop being so scary!"

"I hear you. Let me go ahead and get prepared for my work week ahead...I've got training on Monday that runs for three days, so I want to make sure I have all of my material together to present."

"Okay, love you, and bye cow," Bria replied.

"Bye, cow," Ondrea hung up the phone.

Chapter Seven

It was 6:00 in the AM when Ondrea decided to get up out of her bed, get herself dressed, and prepared for the day ahead, in addition to the conversation she was looking forward to later in the evening with Kamal. She had checked her phone first for any last-minute emails from her supervisor that may have been sent, but instead was pleasantly surprised to find a text from Kamal:

"Good morning, beautiful. This is the day the Lord has made, so make it a great one, and anticipating hearing your voice later."

Once again, Ondrea blushed and replied with a smiling emoji face.

She then grabbed Tania's phone off the charger as she left from her bedroom, and looked down the hallway, heading to the second bedroom door on the right—to make sure Tania was up and getting ready for school in her bathroom.

"Morning, baby girl," Ondrea sang as she knocked on the door before entering.

"Mom, wait—I'm naked!" Tania shrieked as she rushed to cover up her breasts while her mother came into her bedroom.

"I already have the same body parts, Tania Paige," Ondrea stated matter-of-factly as she sat her daughter's phone down on her marble dresser, "I was just making sure you were already up and at 'em."

"Yes mother," Tania sighed as her mother left out of her room. She then quickly put on her underwear and clothing in case she came back in.

Tania did not like her mother barging in on her whenever she felt like it. Furthermore, Tania felt that since she would be turning sixteen next year, she was that much closer to being able to have more independence and freedom from her mother and her cousin Tyrin's tight reigns.

32

The fact that her mother bought her a cell phone, only for her to have to share her passcode and turn it into her before she went to sleep angered Tania. She was an honor student and for the most part, has lived a squeaky-clean life thus far. She had only been to "first base" with a boy before, and over the weekend had her first make-out session and progression to "third base" with her boyfriend of six months, Sebastian—only the most fly freshman at Atlanta International—a private high school that they attended. She loved how he wore his "man bun," and that he favored actor Roshan Fegan from Greenleaf. Sebastian always walked her to and from class and would hold her so close whenever he could between class drop-offs and at lunch…*it was something about being in his arms.*

Londyn was responsible for introducing the couple to each other, and for that reason alone Tania always vowed to look out for Londyn when and if she was ready to entertain boys herself. Londyn had recently developed a crush on Tania's cousin, 'T' who was also the son of Tyrin. Tania hoped for Londyn to find someone else to crush on, but just like his father, T had all the young girls swooning over him wherever he went, and Londyn was not an exception.

Tania hit Londyn up via text asking her to make sure it was okay with her mom that she could start attending cheer tryouts with her for the upcoming basketball season. Tania had overheard Tyrin telling her mother on a Face time that T had tested extremely high on his admission examination, receiving a full-tuition offer at her school, and that he would be starting there with her next week. He would be also be placed in the school's IB program on track for a STEAM endorsement diploma. His exemplary skills in track, football, and basketball from training with Enhance U, also meant he would most definitely be going out for the basketball team—where Sebastian was already the point guard. To Tania, this equaled guaranteed time for the four of them to hang out together. Tania was ecstatic.

"Mom don't forget I have cheer practice after school today, and Ms. Grace is going to drop me off since Londyn is trying out, too," Tania said as she exited her mom's SUV and heading up the front steps of her school.

"Alright," stated Ondrea upon her exit, "have a good day!" she shouted, watching her daughter disappear into the school.

Ondrea missed her "little girl," realizing that she is now three years away from graduating high school and becoming an adult. She wished Chance had been able to see her grow up to this present moment as their daughter would soon need advice as well as "the game" given to her as she started to entertain boys. Her mother's intuition kicked in as Ondrea realized she may need to have Tyrin give her that "game" a little sooner than later. She felt even more comforted in knowing that Tyrin was making legit money now as manager of his uncle's construction firm, which also meant that he was sending his son and namesake, T to the same school as Tania. Not only would he be allowed to have a good experience in the school, but better eyes on Tania to make sure nothing goes awry on her road to success as well.

Ondrea smiled with her eyes looking up towards the sky as she pulled up to her job, *Things are beginning to look up for me God, and I'm open."*

*****

Upon returning to his apartment in Marietta, Kamal had been anticipating his next conversation with Ondrea, since they had hung up the phone from each other that Saturday. When he looked down at his iPhone and saw the time, he could not resist anymore, quickly prayed, and picked up his cell phone to Face time her. He was pleased when she answered the phone on the first ring. Ondrea was wearing a black T-shirt dress with the word, "Faith" on it. Her hair was wrapped up in a black scarf and she had no make-up upon her expresso brown skin—plain Jane—just the way he wanted to see her. *"Man, she's gorgeous,"* he thought to himself.

"Well, hello beautiful," Kamal started off the conversation with a bright smile as he went outside on his balcony to chat.

"Hello, handsome," Ondrea replied as she leaned back in her lounge chair quickly glancing around making sure that nothing was out of place in her living room.

She had purposely made sure that she would not be a temptation this time around with her appearance. Furthermore, she wanted to make sure that they had the best conversation that they were intending to have and one without any interruption. On the other hand, she was distracted by Kamal's beautiful smile, as well as the all-white linen outfit that he was wearing.

"So...let us start by talking about that dress you are wearing," Kamal stated, "are you implying that you now have faith?"

"Dang, you jump right in there, huh? I thought we were supposed to check in with each other to see how our day was until next Monday when we start discussing our weeks?"

"Still trying to dodge me and my questions, I see..."

Ondrea interjected, "...no, I'm not trying to..."

"Well then, you've had a whole day to collect your bearings before our conversation. I hope you don't think because I like you that I'm going to let up on what I'm supposed to discuss with you..."

"No, I'm not saying that, I just wanted to start by telling you how my day was and also interested to hear about yours as well."

"My day was great and got increasingly better once I saw your beautiful face...please tell me that you're starting to have some faith in this world and your walk with Jesus Christ."

Ondrea swallowed the large lump in her throat. If she was going to work at some more relief and deliverance from her past hurt, she had to open up to someone, "to be honest, I have been through so much in my life—from growing up without parents, to losing my daughter's father, amongst other things that have transpired over the years…I just lost hope that anything would be right in my life. That is what made me give up on church and ultimately, God. I felt that He could not love someone like me because of all the things that He had allowed to occur in my life."

"I hate to interrupt your thought, but do you listen to any gospel music by chance?"

"Of course—Kurt Carr, Donald Lawrence, Fred Hammond, William McDowell, Leandria, Zacardi, Koryn, Kierra, and Kirk Franklin are some of my faves and in my playlist…"

"Well, Kirk Franklin's song, 'Just for Me' speaks to the exact feelings that you have in saying "It don't seem fair for you to call this love…" and also backs up the scripture found in Job 13:15 when Job speaks on his feelings surrounding God allowing him all in one day, to be stripped of everything he owned, stricken with a nasty illness similar to leprosy, all of his children died with nothing left but his wife, who in her anger and grief told Job to curse God and die. Instead, Job rebuked his wife and remaining friends who weren't encouraging to him either, and made the bold declaration that although he was grieving and everything had come upon him he still believed the Lord loved him and that he would never stop believing in and serving Him, no matter how much pain he was in."

Ondrea felt the tears well up in her eyes again, but this time she let them fall in front of him on the other side of the camera on her phone, "I'll have to listen to that song then."

Instantly, Kamal felt the need to be at her side and comfort her and immediately was quickened to begin praying for her, "Lord, if I am your true manservant, send comfort to this woman of God for whom I have strong feelings for. Let her feel the presence of Your Holy Spirit as she releases her innermost feelings of

36

hurt anger, and pain to You. Fill her with Your precious Holy Spirit, Lord that she may forever give you all the praise, honor, and worth that is due Your Most Holy Name, in Jesus' name I pray, Amen!"

"Amen," repeated Ondrea, and almost instantly, a calming presence came over her again, and it was then that she was convinced in giving Kamal a chance in helping her to let go, "thank you, Jesus" she whispered as she wiped her tears on her forearm and resumed her posture upright in her lounge chair.

"That's it, Ondrea. Open your mouth and continue to say whatever you feel to our Lord and Savior, Jesus Christ. He's waiting on you to come to Him and give everything to Him in prayer."

"Thank you, Jesus, for your peace, thank you for loving me when I didn't believe You and even gave up on you. Thank You for carrying me and my daughter through in the midst of it all...thank You...thank You...ma-ma-ma-ma..." as she stammered in her words, Ondrea again felt something happen beyond her control, and couldn't fight it—her words began to turn into another language—one in which she didn't understand but could not stop all at the same time. After some minutes had passed, Ondrea felt very tired and thanked Kamal for such a powerful conversation and prayer before excusing herself from their call to gain her composure before Tania arrived back home from cheer practice.

*****

Kamal was a little teary-eyed himself once he heard Ondrea start to speak in tongues. He knew that was God's approval upon how he had conducted himself in conversation with Ondrea during their Facetime. *Thank You, Lord, for hearing my prayer. Thank You for filling her with Your precious gift. Now, direct me in the right way to pursue her as my wife, Lord God. I know now she is who I desire to have grow alongside me on this Christian journey, but I do not want to move outside of Your timing and Your Will,* He prayed to himself after they had hung up.

Chapter Eight

Ondrea could not stop thinking about her encounter with God's Holy Spirit. She had only heard of people speaking in tongues—however, to experience her tongue changing into another language in which she had no control over was outstanding, to say the least. It was now four days from that wonderful first encounter. She wondered how she had sounded to Kamal, but she was too embarrassed to call him up and ask him. She decided to share her exciting news in a group Facetime with her bestie, Bria, and cousin, Marie.

"Hey ladies!" exclaimed Ondrea, waving at the two.

"Hey cow," Bria replied.

"What a pleasant surprise," stated Marie while returning the wave.

"I have a surprise for you guys…"

"…You're dating someone," Marie interjected…

"…I knew you and Minister Davis had a connection…"

"…Wayment…who's Minister Davis, 'Drea?!" asked Marie confused.

Ondrea sighed, "He's one of Dearron's preacher friends, but I am not—and I repeat…not dating that man."

"Have you spent any time with him at all?" Bria asked.

"No! For your information, we only have Facetimed once, and that's what I wanted to talk to you about…"

"Y'all sexting?" Bria continued in her questioning, "'Cause, as much as I have changed, I still wouldn't even be mad at you for finally letting someone in your little bubble."

"Bria, stop!!!" Ondrea yelled at her through the phone.

"I see some people still haven't changed, cuz," Marie added jokingly.

"I'm just saying," retorted Bria, "it's been how long 'Drea gave any man some attention—for a minute I was going to start thinking something else…"

"Okay, Bria I'm warning you," sneered Ondrea in a threatening tone.

"Alright, you two…back to Ondrea's wonderful news she was about to share with us…go on and continue, boo," demanded Marie.

"So, before I was rudely interrupted, I was simply saying that Minister Davis actually had been discussing with me my salvation, and the importance of giving myself completely to God and accepting that He suffers things to happen in our lives for His purpose and that He remains faithful even through the midst of it all."

Marie clapped her hands in a round of applause, "I'm so proud of you for being able to be open with someone enough to counsel about things that have been troubling you…"

"…that's just it, Marie…I still haven't told him anything that has to deal with me other than Tania's father is not with us anymore—he doesn't know in what capacity or anything."

"Dang, 'Drea…are you going to tell him eventually, or see how everything plays out?"

"I just met the man last week! I don't think he needs to know the details of my life story this fast, especially with me not knowing anything about him besides the fact that he's a preacher who says he cannot become a pastor until he finds a wife."

"If that's not a clue or hint, then I don't know what is, cow," said Bria, rolling her eyes.

Ondrea looked to Marie for back-up, however, she gave a thumbs up in Bria's direction, "sorry cousin, but I have to agree with her on that note."

"Y'all ain't right," complained Ondrea, "he's just gonna be my spiritual advisor…now back to my surprise…he helped me to seek the presence of God and His Spirit—I spoke in tongues for the first time, ya'll!"

Both Marie and Bria cheered and jumped up and down on their cameras.

"Yes, cow! I am so happy for you!" exclaimed Bria. "It is so awesome to experience the presence of God. If I could have it my way, I would stay in His presence all the time, but then I know I am someone's wife on top of being a mom, and so I just seize those moments whenever I can. God has been too good to me throughout my crazy days, months, and years of life that I dare not give Him the glory."

"Like Bria said, cousin…I'm incredibly happy for you. This was an awesome surprise." Her doorbell began to ring, "I'll have to talk with you ladies tomorrow, my date is here…"

"Date? Let us see this man," Bria asked.

"I don't know if she wants to be on camera like that…"

"She?!" both Ondrea and Bria exclaimed at the same time.

Marie rolled her eyes and said with confidence, "Yes, I said 'she.'"

Marie felt a big wave of relief come over her when she told her favorite cousin and her cousin's friend that she was dating a woman. Knowing that her cousin gave her life to Christ and that Bria had become the First Lady of a church, Marie was not comfortable with them knowing any details about her personal life—including love interests. She had kept her liking females a secret since high school, but she could not hide it any longer—

especially since things had gotten so serious with Sienna, her current girlfriend. It would only be a matter of time when she would have to introduce her to "the crew."

"Wow," Ondrea replied after a brief silence, "so, how long have you and this girl been dating?"

"It's been about two years…"

"Two years!" both Ondrea and Bria said again in unison. "I know this is a shock, but Bria I didn't know how to break the news to you, and 'Drea, I knew you'd be upset but I didn't feel like being preached to and discussing my personal love life with Sienna to you guys…"

"What you mean? We've told you all of our business!" said Bria visibly upset.

"Yeah, cuz…you had all the tea," Ondrea added.

"I guess you guys are right. I'm not ashamed of her—if that's what you're thinking…"

"You said her name is, Sienna? Bring her by the house sometime, or the four of us all meet up somewhere so we can see what she is all about…how about next weekend, and everyone can come down to the house? 'D has another workshop to attend, so I'll have some free time. 'Drea, bring my 'Taniecey-pooh' and she can watch Noah while we go somewhere and have fun," said Bria.

Marie's eyes widened with joy, "you really mean that Bria?" she asked.

"Of course," Bria replied, "you're still my girl and like family since my bestie is your family. I still love you."

"Yeah Bria, that's a great idea," added Ondrea.

41

"Thanks so much, guys. I will reach back out with you two once I finally talk to her. I love you two, and have a goodnight," Marie stated before hanging up on Facetime.

"Sooooo…. I'm speechless, Bria" said Ondrea.

"I know, right!"

"I'm more surprised that it was your idea to hang out with them."

Bria rolled her eyes, "just because I do not believe that God intended for there to be same-sex couples, does not mean that I still don't want to make sure she isn't in a crappy relationship, just like we would do if it were a guy she was dating."

"Good point," Ondrea stated, "also, how effective would your witness be if you're not 'wise as a serpent and harmless as a dove'."

"Right, so back to Minister Davis and your surprise…"

"Goodbye, cow!" Ondrea said, hanging up on Bria while chuckling to herself, *that girl does not know how to let bygones be bygones…I mean, he's attractive…I mean…okay, he's so doggone sexy it makes no sense, and on top of that he loves God?! Something HAS to be wrong with him…*Ondrea laid across the bed and drifted off into a nap.

Chapter Nine

As Tania and Londyn waited for Ms. Grace to pick them up from cheer practice, they decided to venture over to watch the basketball players practice.

"Look at my man, Sebastian…I got a real one," stated Tania proudly. Her eyes glanced up, down, and across his muscular body as he dribbled the basketball down the court to the hole. When he missed the basket, T backed him up with the rebound and layup into the basket. The remaining cheerleaders and bystanders who were watching, all erupted with cheers for the "new kid in town."

"Tania, what's up with your cousin?" asked Londyn, "He is too fly, and I don't want any other chick to lay claim to him—that's mine," she firmly stated while clutching her Tiffany & Co. heart necklace.

Tania rolled her eyes, "Girl, he has too many females after him—both our age and some nineteen and a twenty-year-olds."

"I don't care how old they are heffa, I'll make him forget all about those broads," Londyn said licking her lips with confidence. T caught and matched her stare with such intensity, she had to look away.

"Girl, did you see the way he just looked at me?!" she squealed while grabbing Tania's arm.

"Girl let me go! You are exaggerating—it wasn't all that."

"Set me out, Tania…Please!"

"Y'all ain't about to have me being an auntie no time soon. Ya'll both have sex on your minds, and you'll be sexing all the time if you two hooked up…I can tell."

"Have you and Sebastian been sexing? Are you holding out on me, heffa because ya'll always hugged up…?"

"Girl, no!" exclaimed Tania, "I'm not ready for all of that yet. I mean, he's been warming it up for me down there…"

"What?!" Londyn exclaimed. "So, you have to give me the details…I can't believe we never discussed this before—it's been like six months since you guys have been together!"

"Well, he's fingered me before, and his head game is fire!" Tania excitedly admitted.

Londyn covered her mouth with shock, "Have you…you know?"

Tania hesitated, "Only once have I tried to return the favor and couldn't do it. He's huge girl, I ain't trying to gag or throw up," she laughed to herself, "he might want to get one of his groupies for all that."

"True, true…well, I want to know what your cousin's mouth do!" she playfully stated, as Tania playfully pushed her back.

"Shut up! Here comes your mom, anyway," she stated as the girls picked up their duffle bags and walked towards her car.

*****

T watched as Tania and Londyn walked out of the basketball gym. He liked what he saw and was curious to know more. Since he started at his new school environment this week, T already had been propositioned to have sex with at least twelve girls ranging from lower class freshman to upper-class senior status and offered head by twice that amount of girls. T knew he had been blessed in many departments. He was a very handsome, athletic, and smart young man, with his father's swag. He chuckled to himself after seeing how bad his cousin's friend was sweating him. *She's so firm…I'll hurt her though—as long as I don't smash I should be straight...* he thought to himself as he walked off the court and headed into the locker room to shower and change.

"Aye Sebastian, what you know about Tania's girl?" asked T.

"Who, Londyn? She's cool...a little dingy, but she doesn't have a lot of miles on her if that's what you wanna know."

"That's what's up, I saw her checking for me, that's all."

"Yeah, Tania mentioned the four of us hooking up for her birthday for bowling or something...you know how girls are playing matchmaker and all," Sebastian replied.

"I mean, she's bad. Especially if my cousin hanging with her, she gotta be official...Tania don't roll with lames."

"You know it, cuz," Sebastian stated.

"Hold up, slow your roll...you might be Tania's nigga, but you, not fam yet, playboy," T told Sebastian playfully but also dead serious at the same time. "You gotta put in some time to earn that 'cuz' title."

"I respect it," Sebastian replied.

The two dapped each other, and T asked Sebastian to go ahead and set him out with Londyn.

"It's done," was all he said in agreement.

Chapter Ten

Ondrea awakened with a startle as she heard her cell phone ring. She looked at the time…1:03 am. *Oh my goodness!* She thought to herself. *Who is calling this late?* She did not recognize the number.

"Hello, may I ask who's calling?" she asked.

"Hey, my beautiful girl," answered Aunt Shelby.

"How are you doing? Is everything okay, Auntie?!" asked Ondrea alarmed.

"Everything's fine, sweetie. I'm sorry to call you so late, however, I wanted to let you know that I just landed in your city tonight, and I'd love to see you before I leave in a couple of days."

"Where are you staying? You know there's room here at the house if you want to stay with me and Tania…"

"Why thank you," replied Aunt Shelby, "I think I will take you up on that offer, young lady."

It had been almost six months since Ondrea had seen her Aunt Shelby, who was also her mother figure and sole caretaker since Ondrea miraculously survived the car crash that killed her parents when she was a baby. Aunt Shelby still traveled the country living off the fruits of her labor as a marketing executive for her own Fortune 500 company.

"So, when can I expect you, or do I need to grab you from the airport?"

"Nonsense, I am going to get a Lyft in the morning to your house—it's late."

"You must be with one of your 'boos' then…" Ondrea fished for an answer.

"Girl, hush, and I'll see you later on this morning," Aunt Shelby replied.

"Okay, I'll go and start getting your room ready, just let me know when you pull up so I can let you in," Ondrea stated before hanging up the phone.

Ondrea sent a text to her supervisor letting them know she'd be in later that day, sat up on the side of the bed, and waited one minute before getting out of the bed to start sprucing up the place. Knowing her aunt, she would be there bright and early before Tania got up to get ready for school. She made sure to lay out the Kate Spade towels on the bed downstairs in the guest bedroom and made sure her welcome tray on the nightstand was stocked with Aunt Shelby's favorites: Black soap, Perrier water, and soft peppermint candy whenever she stayed there. Ondrea took great pride in taking care of her Aunt and any others who stayed in her home.

Sure enough, as soon as the clock struck seven o'clock, the phone rang, and Ondrea was there to greet her aunt with open arms.

"Good morning, sunshine!" She rang out, hugging Ondrea back.

"I'm so glad to see you...let me get your things and make you some breakfast...Tania already left for school, but we can surprise her later when she gets out of cheer practice."

"Alright, my dear," replied Aunt Shelby as she hugged Ondrea tightly and kissed her on the cheek.

Ondrea made the two of them some Belgian waffles, bacon, grits, and scrambled eggs before getting ready herself to leave for work.

"I completely forgot how great your waffles tasted, my dear," stated Aunt Shelby.

"Thanks so much. I mix a lot of love in it," Ondrea replied.

"So, tell me my dear...what's been up? How's life treating you so far?" Aunt Shelby asked while chewing another bite of her waffles.

Ondrea sighed, "It's going…I mean the job is going well, I'm trying to raise that great-niece of yours in addition to trying to approach life a little more different this time."

"How so?"

"Well, while I was visiting with Bria and Dearron and their new son, they had me attend one of the revivals at their church, and the guest preacher ended up praying for me. He told me things that I never shared with anyone, and we've been communicating ever since. He said that he wants me to gain my faith and trust back in the Lord and grow more spiritually. At first, I was hesitant about making that move, but he had me listen to a song called, 'Just for Me' and it's helped me see things from a different perspective than the rationale I had in my head. God is still faithful no matter the storms in life and/or situations He suffers us to go through."

"Preach!" exclaimed Aunt Shelby, "Are you going back to church now? You should maybe join that man's church…what's his name?"

"Slow down, Auntie," chuckled Ondrea.

"His name is Minister Kamal Davis, and he's from Marietta, Georgia. I've agreed to just talk with him on Mondays, and there's something else…"

"He wants to marry you?" Aunt Shelby cut her off.

"No! No way…"

"Honey, the man is interested in courting you…trust me, I know these things."

"Auntie, with all due respect, I've never known you to be in love with anyone or ever married—engaged for that fact."

Aunt Shelby shifted nervously in her seat before reaching across the table to grab Ondrea's hands, "look me dead in my eyes, sweetie," she said.

Ondrea obeyed and did so.

"When I was twenty-two years old, I met this man named Bernard Jackson at a Babyface concert. We hit it off instantly and became awfully close lovers and friends. He always wanted more from me and even wanted to marry me, but I was too scared to give my all to a man when I saw all my friends one-by-one get their hearts broken by the men they swore were upstanding and spoiled them with gifts but cheating on them multiple times in the process with their family members and other friends they associated with. I vowed to be nothing like them…to maintain my strength and not allow the weakness (or so I thought was a weakness) in loving a man exclusively to take root…"

"So, what happened next?" asked Ondrea curiously.

"I pushed him away and rejected all of his advances after that, and eventually never returned his phone calls and letters."

"We call that 'ghosting', Auntie," informed Ondrea.

"What you said…" her voice trailed off, and she began to look away when she started tearing up, "…I loved him, you know," she sobbed while wiping away her tears.

"Don't cry," Ondrea said as she got up from the table to embrace her Aunt. Her mother. The one who represented so much strength now was in her face showing so much vulnerability.

49

"That man loved me in spite of me and was so patient…he died while he was writing me another letter!" she exclaimed and buried her face in Ondrea's bosom while weeping uncontrollably.

"Oh, Auntie!" Ondrea held her even tighter until her crying subsided.

"So, you see why I have nothing but an empty life—no love—just travel," Aunt Shelby began to explain while wiping the tears away once more. "I escape from my pain by traveling here and there, Ondrea. If you don't allow love to find its way into your heart again, you'll be doing the same. Right now, your void is Tania. She's getting older and will leave you soon. If this man is pouring into you, and sowing into you godly things, then you can't ask for anything better than that. I'm not saying that he must be perfect, but any man who genuinely loves God and wants to be pleasing in His sight will have no choice but to operate in ways that please you."

Ondrea hugged and thanked her Aunt Shelby for the honest talk and advice shared and informed her that she would be back after work to pick her up, ride to grab Tania from practice, and then out to eat.

*****

Five more days, and we get to talk again, Ondrea thought to herself before she pulled out of the driveway staring down at her iPhone in her hand. She wanted to continue to get to know Kamal and share more about her in return, but at the same time, she continued to have her reservations. *Am I ready to pursue a relationship with this man? Should I just keep it strictly friends? 'Drea, you don't even fully know him and who he is…learn from your mistakes,"* she advised herself. It was the confirmation that she needed to be able to accept what she already knew to be true in her heart.

~Meanwhile across towns~

As he locked up the church and began to walk to his 2020 Cadillac XT6, Kamal's mind wondered what Ondrea was doing. He knew that they agreed to only communicate on Mondays, but she was constantly on his mind. Every time she crossed it, he prayed for her, and him—that God calms his spirit concerning her. He picked up his phone, considered texting her, and then put it back down. *Temperance, brotha*, he told himself.

Chapter Eleven

The weekend came and went, and Ondrea could not be any more excited than a kid in a candy store. It was now the third Monday that she and Kamal had been having their weekly conversations, and she was looking forward to this one. She decided to send a "Good morning" text to him first, this time.

"Good morning, man of God. I look forward to hearing your voice and seeing you later. Have a blessed day." She hit send and smiled at her initiating a romantic gesture for a change. It felt right.

"Lord, I thank You for this day and thank you for the visit with Aunt Shelby and sending confirmation that You are doing some things for me. Thank You for keeping my daughter and me through these years, this week, and even in this hour. I ask that You bless everyone attached to me. Continue to deal with me in a mighty way, and I am open to receive everything that You have for me. I give myself to You, Lord. In Jesus' name, Amen."

On her way to work, she blasted William McDowell's "I Give Myself Away," and sung it at the top of her lungs. She was ready to give her all.

*****

Ondrea could not wait for her workday to end. She decided to call Minister Davis first and not wait around another minute. She applied some of her Top-Secret lip gloss from Brittney Kelley Brands "Chic Girl" line and smoothed out her deep wave curls in her hair with some finger combs.

"Hello, lady," he answered as he accepted the FaceTime. He was dressed in a Khaki-colored Lacoste hooded short tracksuit.

"Hey, handsome, I'm loving that look on you," she replied flirtatiously while biting her bottom lip. She liked what she saw and was secretly praying to God to help her not flirt so much.

"Let me call you right back, I need to pray first…"

"…Are you serious?" Ondrea interjected.

"Dead serious," he firmly replied.

He had to take back control of the conversation. *"Lord, cover me and allow me to die out, so that You may be lifted up in this conversation. Gird me up so that I may resist any temptation and remain totally focused on representing You and Your Spirit in the right manner. In Jesus' name, Amen."*

Kamal dialed Ondrea back, and this time with some strength, "Hello, Ms. Ondrea, I apologize for the inconvenience, but I wasn't ready," he chuckled.

"I understand, Minister Davis," she replied. "I will try to be more mindful not to test you…So, the reason I initiated on today is that while I've been opening up some about me, meanwhile I don't know much about you—the man who has been the occupier of my time and attention on Monday now for the second week…"

"I see," he responded. "I understand where you are coming from. Maybe I can fill you in after our weekly report…"

"…You see, that's what has been on my mind this week—who are you?"

"What you mean?" he shifted in his chair with curiosity.

"I mean, the encounter that we both had on the altar, and prayer that you prayed over me, not to mention the chemistry…yet I know nothing about you other than you are telling me you have no baby mama drama and a dark past."

"I do not wish to discuss my past and what I used to do, because it may scare you away from pursuing anything with me further than where we are right now."

"But I thought your past would be a testimony and therefore encouraging and something to brag on God about how he brought you out…"

"…It's not that simple. I wish it were," he lamented.

"Just like your love life is complicated, so is my past. When you let me in about that, I will let you in on mine," he stated matter-of-factly.

Ondrea knew she had struck a nerve with him, so she decided to ask Kamal about how he knew he was called to ministry. He told her that he was participating in some illegal business, and he heard the voice of the Lord audibly, asking him if this was the life he wanted to continue to live. He then informed her that on that night he pleaded with God to get him out of "the life" alive, and he would serve Him all the days of his life.

"It was then that I knew after God brought me out, that my mission in life was to help other young men overcome the street life and all that comes with it."

"That's awesome, Minister Davis," Ondrea stated. "I love how God spoke to you in your sin and basically called you out."

"Just like He's called you out of your bitterness and anger, Ondrea…we aren't that much different in some respects."

"I guess so," she agreed.

He couldn't wait any longer—he knew it was the right timing, "come visit my church this weekend, Ondrea. I'd love to be the one to baptize you—that is if you're ready."

"I…I don't know if I'm ready for being baptized, but I'll come and visit."

"What has you so apprehensive about being baptized?"

"I don't know, it just seems so final—like once I go down in 'Jesus' name,' that there's no coming back from that. I know my life and all that it represented for the past fifteen going on sixteen years will change into meaning something new."

"Change is scary, but that's where your faith is supposed to kick in, and you trust that God has something good in store for all of the trials and tribulations you've had to endure."

"Okay, Minister Davis—hold up," Ondrea suddenly shifted the conversation, "you didn't tell me what your thoughts were last week."

"True," he replied. "I have had trouble sleeping all this week trying to plan this upcoming bible study series on faith and operating in our measure of faith that God personally gives us."

"That's pretty cool."

"Yeah, the only thing I hate about preparing lessons is the time—or loss thereof that occurs. I'm always so drained whenever I'm planning things of this seriousness."

"Well, I am supposed to visit with Bria this weekend, so if you are finished with your series by the time, I get back from hanging out with her, then maybe we could catch some lunch before Sunday, or dinner after you preach...of course, you know that's a long drive just to come and grab me..." *Did I just let that come out of my mouth?!* Ondrea wanted to beat herself up for offering so much too fast. This forwardness was all new to her, and she did not know how to turn it off. She prayed again, *"Lord, help me."*

Kamal cut her off, "That sounds like a plan, I'll make sure I let you know, lady…have a good night, and may God bless you until we see and talk to each other again..."

"…Amen and Amen, in Jesus' name," Ondrea stated as she ended Minister Davis' prayer. "Goodnight."

Chapter Eleven

Tania was missing Sebastian already, as she and her mother were riding down the highway to her godparent's house for the weekend. She had not seen them in almost a year, and was eager to meet Jonoah, and spend time with them. Bria was cool, but strict at the same time, while Dearron was the father figure that she never had. Tania longed for her father and mourned the relationship that she never was able to experience with him. It was Dearron who helped her learn how to ride a bicycle without training wheels, take her to father-daughter dances while she was growing up, in addition to spoiling her with gifts every holiday and birthday. If it were not for her mother's love and care, she would have opted to live with them instead. *"They wouldn't be so overbearing with me for sure!"*

"Penny for your thoughts?" asked Ondrea.

Tania snapped out of her daze and turned to face her mother, "Oh, it's nothing mom, I'm just a little sleepy."

"You probably should go to bed at a decent time, and not be on the phone so much…I know you've been sneaking it out of my room, Tania…"

"Mom, I'm sorry," she confessed.

"Save it, Tania…I was your age once…I know," Ondrea acknowledged her daughter's need for communication outside of school, "who are you talking to that late on the phone anyway? Is it that boy, Sebastian?"

"Mom, he's a good guy and respects me."

"I didn't ask for all of that information, I asked is that who you've been talking to?"

"Him and 'T mom... 'T knows Sebastian and I go together, and he's very protective of me, like Cousin Tyrin," Tania rolled her eyes and said matter-of-factly.

"I don't care, Tania...you have to be careful of your conversations with boys when it's that late at night...you two can start off innocent, but it can lead to something totally left, and next thing you know you two will be—if not already—having phone sex."

"Mom!" Tania exclaimed in embarrassment, "we don't do stuff like that!"

"Well, that's good to hear, but still watch out for it. Promise me that you will let me know when you start thinking about having sex..."

Tania could not believe her mother was going there right now, but Ondrea knew it was the right moment to talk to Tania—mother-to-daughter and keep it real with her about sex. She swallowed hard, and continued, "I fell 'head over heels' in love with your father after the first date and also my first-time having sex..."

"You had sex with dad on the first date?!" Tania interrupted with a shocked expression across her face.

"Unfortunately, yes I did. I wish I hadn't because sex blinds you to a lot of red flags or other things you need to pay attention to while dating someone and making sure that you want to even be serious with the individual—let alone take it to the next level."

"I hear you mom, but I'm not ready for that, and Sebastian hasn't pressured me either to do anything."

Ondrea continued to give her daughter some more advice, "Make sure that he doesn't, because if he is doing that…he can't care about you all that much. That is called being selfish. Since you will be sixteen soon, I have decided to go ahead and trust you to make the right decisions when it comes to relationships. Just promise me you will let me know…"

"Yes ma'am, I hear you," Tania replied excitedly, "thank you so much, mom."

It was in that moment that Tania wished her mother and her were closer so that she could feel comfortable opening up to her and letting her know that she was indeed thinking of letting Sebastian be her first and giving it up to him on either Homecoming night, or better yet—on her birthday. She wanted to take heed to her mother's warning about avoiding making a wrong move—after all, her father was a drug dealer who ended up being murdered before she was born…*I better listen to my mother. I do not want to end up like her being alone with having the task of raising a child.*

*****

"Look at how long your hair has grown!" Bria said while hugging Tania, "Hey cow, glad you made it back down this way."

"Thanks, Auntie, mom won't let me cut it," Tania lamented.

"Yeah, I had to come and see about some things, if you know what I mean," Ondrea hinted to Bria about their girl's night, who just nodded for confirmation.

"Well, Tania let me show you to your room, and 'Drea you remember where yours is, right?"

Ondrea nodded yes. Of course, she remembered the room where everything changed the moment Minister Davis aka Kamal came knocking on the door. Ondrea was nervous to tell Bria about agreeing to go to Kamal's church for service on Sunday. He was to pick her up on Saturday and bring her to Marietta, where she would stay overnight at a separate location—"details following"—he had told her. She knew Bria would not let her live it down and will want to grill her afterward for all details. She will find a way to break the news later, but for now, she just wanted to concentrate on having fun with the girls.

Tania took instantly to Jonoah, and it did not take much convincing or coercing to get her to agree to watch him that evening. Later, she and the girls were going to catch up with each other, as they had discussed—the only tag-along would be Bria's friend, Taylor. Taylor's husband was going to the same convention Dearron was, so it was only right Bria thought to call and include her in their festivities for the evening.

*****

Ondrea could see how Taylor and Bria became so cool and in the same circle because Taylor once was where Bria was. Her husband, forty-six-year-old, and Rockmond Dunbar look-alike Bishop Charles Kinsley III was the pastor of a huge mega-church and had been known to be notably argued as one of the best preachers in the Atlanta-area. Being the daughter of an Apostle and only thirty-three herself, Taylor had already been familiar with the makings of being a Pastor's wife—not to forget to include how to handle the ups and downs that come along with being able to help aid other women in the ministry who are single or married in how to walk with God and effectively cultivate their homes while also being an exemplary wife. The downs came from the criticism she had faced by not having any children yet with her husband, in addition to the many women who were attracted to her husband's calling and anointing and wanted to be with her husband. Learning how to navigate through all these scenarios caused Taylor to be much more mature than most females and wives at her age.

Five years ago, when Taylor had heard of the "new" pastor's wife who was fighting other women that wanted her husband, she knew she was called to help this woman—Bria Jackson—and they had been "homegirls" since.

"Hey ladies," Taylor called out to both Bria and Ondrea as she got into the backseat of Bria's 2021 Lexus NX.

"Hey," they both replied in unison.

"Your outfit is fly!" Bria exclaimed as she eyed Taylor's navy sequined-kimono-sleeved ASOS jumpsuit, "you sure your hubby knows what you're wearing?" she jokingly added.

"Please, chica—I represent him wherever I step out, so you know I have to match his flyy…" Taylor said as she flipped her long, brown hair in the night wind.

"Talk to'em, chica," Bria cut in, "we all look fly tonight," she said as she also took note of her own silver One33 Beaded-fringe halter dress and Ondrea's blue Gucci-belted romper.

"So, where we headed?" Taylor asked.

"Rocks on the Roof," answered Bria while turning to look at Ondrea, "if I want to just get away 'Drea, this is where we go to have some wine and relax—it's so low-key."

"Okay, cool," Ondrea replied.

"Is your cousin still meeting us there?" asked Taylor, "Bria mentioned to me the 4-1-1, so I wouldn't be surprised or cause any awkwardness in front of her and her friend."

"As far as I know, Bria told me that she would set everything up since I'm not all the way familiar with this city, and its hot spots…It's cool, Taylor, thanks for letting me know that" Ondrea replied.

Marie was growing more nervous by the minute, "Babe, what's taking you so long?" she asked

Sienna as she finished buttoning the last button on her black see-through Dolce & Gabbana Tie-neck,

polka dot blouse.

Sienna emerged from the bathroom in a matching print romper from Kate Spade and Altruistic frames.

She was also nervous to meet Marie's favorite cousin, in addition to their friend who was a pastor's wife. Both

she and Marie have been through a lot of scrutiny and judgment since they had decided to come out publicly as

a couple. Both Marie and Sienna's parents' relationships with them were strained as a result, not to mention the

shame and dirty looks they receive whenever they wanted to attend a church service.

"Babe, I don't know if I can do it," Sienna said.

Marie could sense her fear, "We've waited two whole years to do this, come on babe," she

reassured Sienna with a loving embrace.

*****

"This place is so bomb," Ondrea stated as they walked to their seating area.

"I know, right!" exclaimed Taylor.

"Where's your cousin and her girl?" Bria asked.

"Right behind you," Marie said as both she and Sienna approached the table together.

"Hey cuz," Ondrea stated, "I'm so happy to see you in person…" she said while hugging her

cousin. Her eyes shifted to the woman her cousin was holding hands with, "…you must be Sienna?" she asked

extending her hand.

Sienna shook her hand and everyone else's in their company, "I am and it's nice to meet you

guys."

62

"Finally!" exclaimed Marie playfully. She was happy and knew that after the warm greeting, the night was going to be okay.

"I haven't had this much fun in a group setting in a long time…thanks so much for letting us hang out with you guys," said Sienna.

"Anytime," said Bria.

"Yeah," added Ondrea, "your sense of humor is crazy-hilarious…we all have to link up more often…it was very nice to meet you, Sienna."

"Thanks so much, guys," Marie answered for Sienna while staring at Taylor's face and searching for her thoughts.

Taylor remained silent.

Sensing the awkwardness, Bria quickly intervened. "Well, it's getting late and we're gonna have to start heading back ladies before Tania calls for me to get my baby…again, it was nice to meet you Sienna, and we'll have to plan another outing sooner than later," she added while shooting Taylor a nasty look.

*****

"What was that all about, Taylor?" asked Bria.

Taylor shifted around uncomfortably in the backseat and refused to look Bria's way.

"Taylor…is there something you want to share with us that has you so wacky and out of sorts?"

"You have to promise that what I tell you does not leave this car, ladies," Taylor said while finally looking ahead at Bria and Ondrea.

"Okay, we promise," both replied in unison.

63

"Sienna and I had a relationship back when I was about twenty-one…"

"Swear!" exclaimed Ondrea.

"The Bible tells us not to swear, Ondrea," stated Taylor, "… it's not something that I'm proud of, but it's one of the experiences in my life that made me and has helped develop my walk and testimony."

"This is true, my friend," agreed Bria. "So…how long did you two date? What was it like?"

"I knew the questions would come…we went together for about two months, and it was cool for the experience that it was, however, I broke up with her when I met my husband…She was very attentive to me and my body, but that's all it was…Charles is that for me and much more. Most importantly, he feeds my soul and has helped me mature so much in God."

"Wow… well we all have skeletons and wild times in our closets," chimed in Bria. "I thank God our husbands found us when they did!" exclaimed Bria. Ondrea already knew Bria's dark secrets…how she was adopted at sixteen by foster parents after her biological mother sold her into sex trafficking at the age of fourteen for a heroin fix. Bria had encounters with both males and females during that horrible time—done things sexually that no young girl should ever have to perform and participate in. Dearron was Bria's high school sweetheart, and it was nothing but the grace of God that kept her.

"Thank you, ladies, for not judging me," Taylor said as Bria pulled up into her driveway. "It was so awkward seeing her, in addition to keeping my composure in front of your cousin, Ondrea."

"I can only imagine," stated Ondrea.

Taylor closed the back door and the two watched to make sure that she was safe in her home before pulling off.

"So…I definitely was not expecting this kind of revelation on tonight."

"I am not surprised 'Drea. You already know the life I come from…I've learned to never judge a book by its cover."

"True…so, tomorrow Minister Kamal is going to pick me up from your house, and drive me down there to Marietta to hear him preach on Sunday…"

"Really now!" exclaimed Bria. "So, are you staying with him, or—"

"—I'm staying in a separate arrangement—"

"…Right!" said Bria sarcastically, "girl, that man is about to make you his wife!"

Ondrea brushed Bria's comment off, "I'm going down there to hear him preach for Sunday service—that's it and that's all."

"Yeah, alright," Bria stated. "Well, I suppose you'd like for me to keep Tania occupied?"

"Darn, I forgot all about that part," Ondrea lamented.

"Don't worry, you owe me," Bria said playfully as they began to pull into her garage.

"I'm scared to even ask…"

"You owe me a FULL report upon your return! Just let me know when you guys are on your way back on Sunday, and I'll make sure either myself or D takes Tania out somewhere."

Chapter Twelve

Since she was only riding in the car with Kamal on tomorrow, she wanted to make sure she would be cute and comfy and packed in her additional overnight bag, a green aviator "Babe" jumpsuit from Fashion Nova. She decided that she would pull her hair up into a high ponytail and accessorize it with traditional gold hoop earrings and her gold Michael Kors sneakers. As she began to put on her pajamas, and get ready for bed, she checked her iPhone:

"Good evening, lady. I wanted to make sure it is still okay for me to pick you up from D and Bria's house tomorrow?"

Ondrea smiled, and texted back: **"Good evening, sir...I am packed and ready...what time should I be expecting you?"**

"Since it's a four-hour drive, I figured I'd come between noon and one o'clock...that way we'd both have some time to chill out and relax before the morning."

"Cool with me, Minister Kamal."

Ondrea put her phone on the charger, and with a smile on her face, drifted off to sleep.

In the morning....

"Good morning, beautiful. It's looking more like one o'clock for ETA."

"Okay, thanks for the heads up."

Kamal made sure that he prayed and fasted before he gassed up and hit the road for the long drive. He had to be able to maintain his composure, as well as have temperance in dealing with Ondrea. *Please let her be decent in dress and conversation, Lord. Help me to remember You and the way that You would have for me to conduct myself in her presence. In Jesus' name, I pray, Amen.*

*****

Bria had taken Tania with her to Abercorn Walk—an outdoor shopping mall, to shop until they dropped, and then to the movies for a God mom and God-daughter day. Ondrea paced around the room until she received the text that Kamal was outside.

Remember to keep cool 'Drea, she told herself. *It is just a car ride and church in the morning.*

Kamal watched as Ondrea came out in her jumpsuit carrying her Louis Vuitton overnight bag with the matching garment bag. *She can wear anything and look like a million bucks,* he thought to himself as he watched her smile, wave, and proceed to walk towards the car. Kamal quickly snapped out of his gaze and got out of the car to grab her overnight bag, place it in the trunk and open the passenger-side door. He then instructed her to have a seat in his car, while he put her garment bag in the backseat on the hook above the door. *Lord, again please take control and let me die out so you can get the glory out of this conversation.* Every time he was around her, he felt like this. Kamal had been with hundreds of women over his lifetime before accepting his call to ministry and never looked back…He did not understand why it was so tempting to "risk it all" with Ondrea though. *Reel it in, brotha,* he repeated to himself before getting into the car.

The burgundy suit with chocolate brown accents is what was doing it for Ondrea. She loved the fact that Kamal dressed dapper and debonaire all the time. Every time she saw him dressed to the nines; he made her want to match his fly.

"Do you always dress up every day?" she asked him as he backed out of the driveway and began the drive to Marietta.

Kamal chuckled to himself, "Every day that I have business to attend to with the church, the answer is yes…and what about you? Are you always this fly when you step out? And no blue at that…What's up with that?"

"I didn't think this was that 'fly,' but thanks…blue is not the only color I like. So, what do you wear on those days that you don't have to be all 'fly'?"

"I love to lounge in Faceup and T.R.A.P. apparel, tracksuits…Nike is my brand of choice. What is your preference?"

"Well, I love my high-end clothes like Dolce & Gabbana, but I also love clothes

from Kaydense Galleria and cheap finds from Theze-Dealz thrift store for leisure, and DKNY for suits when I go to work…I also like to lounge in just jumpsuits like these," Ondrea stated.

"Okay, okay…" Kamal stated coolly.

The two of them carried on in casual conversation for another half an hour, before the mellow, smooth jazz sounds from Kamal's SIRIUS XM Radio caused Ondrea to drift off to sleep for about another hour and a half. She began to wake up once Kamal stopped at Chic-fil-A's drive-thru for a quick bite to eat. After eating in the car, Ondrea decided to liven up their drive a little.

"So…who wants to play random questions?" Ondrea asked. This way, she felt they both could learn more about each other on the way to Marietta.

"Okay, I'm game...go ahead...shoot," said Kamal.

"Alrighty. If you have never played this game before, you have to remember not to ask a question that you cannot answer for yourself. So, for starters, who's your favorite male and female singer?"

"Dead or alive?" Kamal asked for clarity.

"It can be either/or," Ondrea answered.

"Male singer would have to be Donnie Hathaway and female would have to be Whitney Houston...no one can touch her...what's yours?"

"My favorite male singer hands down is Tank...love him! Female singer is Patti Labelle for me..."

"You know Tank used to be a worship leader before he went secular?"

"I heard about that...I would love it if he went back to gospel, also...what about your favorite celebrity crush?"

"Tika Sumpter, the actress from Tyler Perry's Haves and Have Nots...now, she's fire."

"Okay, okay...I reply to you in return by saying that I love me some Hosea Chanchez, also known as "Malik" from The Game."

"Alright, um...what's your actual favorite color?"

Ondrea smiled, "Blue...yours?"

"Black—"

"What?!" Ondrea interrupted, "I just knew you'd say a lighter color since you are always so optimistic and preaching about faith…"

"You would think, but some theologians argue that the color black's spiritual meaning is the sign of the Holy Spirit, and also the color of Pentecost—or the outpouring of God's Spirit on the Apostles."

"I'll need a Bible Study on that, Mr…" Ondrea replied playfully. "Anyway, back to our question game…I'm upping the ante a little...tell me about your parents, and like what kind of child you were."

"Dang, you just dive right in, huh?" Kamal cleared his throat. *Welp here goes nothing…* he thought to himself.

"Remember, I have to answer the same question after you…"

"True…okay… I never knew who my father was because he was serving a life sentence for drug trafficking on top of murdering two people, and he ended up getting stabbed up and died while he was incarcerated. My mother raised me until I was about fifteen…she was hardly home sometimes because she was always gone on drug binges. There were always men who came in and out of the house. Not having any structure left me open to all of Satan's tactics. Because I was left to care for my own well-being, I ended up following in my father's footsteps—or so I was told—when I left home and started selling drugs with my boy."

"What kind of drugs did you sell?" Ondrea asked.

"Heroin, cocaine, weed…you name it. Our operation was solid, and I had made a lot of money throughout the years from the business…now, your turn, lady."

Ondrea gathered her thoughts. *She wanted to know more…*

"What about school for you?"

"I thought you could only ask me one question at a time, and then you answer the same one?"

"I know, but this is a part of your childhood, so it still applies," she added matter-of-factly.

"I see…you like to make up your own rules…that's cool," he teased. "I'll continue to play along with your little game…" Kamal shifted up in the driver's seat and replied in a more serious tone, "I was an honor student up until one of my mom's boyfriends, a distributor, recruited me and my boy to start working with him. I loved participating in sports, science fairs—I loved it all," he smiled to himself.

The smile quickly faded just as fast as it appeared, "that is until he had us carrying and dropping off drugs for him. What turned into an after-school activity, grew into a rather lucrative business for all of us as his client base grew, and demand for the product did all at the same time. We were expected to keep up with the demand, and at that point, school became secondary…at thirty, I ended up going back through a high school credit recovery program and earned my diploma…I just finished up last year with my bachelor's degree in Criminal Justice from Georgia State University."

"That's an awesome testimony, Minister Kamal," expressed Ondrea.

Kamal was immensely proud of himself and how God's grace had covered and protected him while he was active in "the life." He was indeed a changed man.

"Okay, Lil' lady…your turn…" he reminded Ondrea of her turn to answer the question.

71

I knew this was coming. "Sooo…my parents died in a car accident on their way to their high school prom, and I was somehow delivered and miraculously survived."

Kamal glanced over at Ondrea in amazement, "That's a message within itself…the purpose that is tied to your life…wow, I just got chills from hearing you say this...please, keep going…" he urged.

Ondrea obliged, "My Aunt Shelby ended up raising me, and I was also an honor student through high school. Interestingly, you and I have some similarities in growing up with no structure—my Aunt, escaping her own issues and life, traveled constantly—which left me home alone many weekends during my junior and senior years. I received a full-ride to Spelman College for Psychology, but after some life changes, I transferred to Emory to complete the Postdoctoral Forensic Psychology program."

Smart AND accomplished? "I'm just blown away at your testimony. You have persevered a lot in the short thirty-three years of your life…you inspire me," Kamal added.

"Why thank you, Minister Kamal," replied Ondrea humbly, "I would like to thank God for his covering and protection…except for the one thing he never shielded me from…"

"Like?" Kamal urged Ondrea to continue to express her feelings.

"Let me guess, you're gonna make this my question?"

"Of course," he added.

Ondrea playfully hit Kamal in his leg jokingly.

"Don't mess with a man while he's operating heavy machinery," he added playfully to lighten up the mood. "You better be glad this is our exit. I'm gonna have you to stop there, but trust we'll finish this conversation after church tomorrow."

Kamal hated asking her such an uncomfortable question, however, he knew that this question was crucial to not only her healing, but his way of learning more about her pain, and how he might be of assistance to help.

He then pulled into the parking lot and entryway into the Four Seasons Hotel. All these years that Ondrea lived in the area, she had never been inside this beautiful establishment. Returning to his car after checking Ondrea bags into her room at the front desk and finally handing her the key, Ondrea was impressed where he was putting her up, and how he was handling her. She could already tell that he was very protective—another trait Chance had possessed—with their similar backgrounds, she wondered what it was about her that attracted these guys that were from the streets or had that as a part of their background. If Kamal had not turned his life around, she would not give him the time of day either. *I can't go back down that road of disappointment.*

"Alright, Minister Kamal," Ondrea stated expressing her gratitude as she prepared to get out of his car and walk inside to her room. "I appreciate you having me stay here."

"Well, I definitely can't have you staying with me at my place, on top of making sure that any woman I have an interest in has to be treated with the utmost respect and class. Speaking of that, you have both spa and room service already taken care of if you choose to use them the rest of today or bright and early in the morning before a car will come and pick you up for service—unfortunately, I won't be able to pick you up due to me having to prepare for service at the church."

"Wow, I thank you again for this, Minister Kamal. Have a great night."

Hearing Kamal say this to her started to excite her and she had to remind herself again not to flirt with him, and reel it back in.

"Again, I appreciate it, and look forward to experiencing the service tomorrow."

"Alright, lady," he replied before pulling off after watching her walk inside the hotel.

*****

Ondrea opened the door to her deluxe city-view room with her digital key code Kamal had given her and was so pleased with the view. At 6:30 pm, she went to her Happy Hour Spa Treatment appointments that were already scheduled: De-stress Massage and the Four Seasons Signature Manicure Spa Services. *He thinks he is slick!* She thought to herself. He made her think the services were optional…Instead of bothering him while he might be studying or concentration on tomorrow, Ondrea fought the urge to contact him.

*****

Kamal lay awake in his bed. He checked the time…1:15 AM. He did not know why he was so restless. *Lord, whatever it is calm my spirit so I can get rest and be ready to deliver your Word later this morning. In Your name, I pray, Amen.*

Chapter Thirteen

Ondrea made sure that she was awake, dressed, checked out, and ready downstairs by the time Kamal's assistant came to pick her up. She had spritzed herself with some Bond No. 9's Scent of Peace and was already causing heads to turn while she waited for her ride. She was wearing her pink Dolce & Gabbana Cady ¾ sleeve pencil dress, along with matching polka shoes, purse as well as matching pearl necklace and earring set. Her newly manicured nails made the outfit pop even more—she was so glad she had gotten a pedicure the weekend before. Ondrea still had her hair up in a bun to have her pearls stand out even more.

As Kamal's assistant, Bryan pulled the car up to get her, even he did a double-take when Ondrea came outside. *Man, she is beautiful...* He had thought to himself; *I know Minister better wife that for sure!*

They pulled up at Destiny to Faith Deliverance Ministries. Ondrea remembered seeing the name of that ministry someplace before, and immediately she felt an overwhelming sense of anxiousness as she got out of the car, thanked Bryan, and proceeded to head up the front steps, of the church. As she arrived inside, Ondrea quickly located where the bathroom was and made sure she had freshened up and used the restroom before service was to start. As she made her way into the vestibule and entryway into the sanctuary, Ondrea stopped to sign in at the visitor's book.

"Ms. Ondrea Williams?" an older lady called out to Ondrea.

"That's me...I'm Ondrea," she replied with a puzzled look on her face.

"Minister Davis is expecting you. I know you're his guest on today," she warmly stated and reached out for a hug.

Ondrea hugged the woman back wondering who she was. Her expression must have told exactly what she was feeling.

"My name is Helen, and I am one of the mothers here at the church…now everyone doesn't know that, but he trusts me in confidence to make sure that you felt welcomed among strangers."

This man doesn't cease to amaze me, Ondrea thought to herself and smiled. "I appreciate you and the hospitality you are already showing me, Ms. Helen…I'm truly at a loss for words."

"Just know you're someone special because I haven't had him come to me about a woman in some years…I was starting to get worried about him," she added in a joking manner. "Come on, beautiful, and let us get a good seat before this sanctuary fills up.

Ms. Helen picked out seats for her and Ondrea in the third row upfront. Ondrea could feel the stares— some of the jealousy and some of the simple curiosity on who the mysterious and beautiful woman was who came to visit their service this morning.

*****

A few more minutes had passed before the choir began to march in, and the order of service began. After the choir sang a couple of selections, out from the back of the church walks Kamal, and he continued walking up into the pulpit dressed in a black preacher's robe with Red trim. As he went to sit down after praying, he spotted Ondrea seated next to Mother Helen. Kamal gave a quick smile, asked for the congregation to welcome its visitors, and speak to each other in acknowledgment, and continued with his portion of the service by raising an offering.

His message was, "Damaged Goods: Salvaged for Purpose," with his key text coming from Matthew 16:17-18; Galatians 2:20; Psalms 34:18.

"All of us are born into this world and shaped in iniquity (or sin)," Kamal started. I hope ya'll don't mind me teaching ya'll a little something on this morning," he added. "Sin is what leads to destruction and death. When you look up the word "Damage" in Webster's dictionary it means, "to inflict physical harm on (something) to impair its value, usefulness or normal function."

He continued, "Some of us have grown up with no cares in the world as a child, while others have had it rough coming up. Some of us have had things done to us (violated at early ages) and may also have had things like sickness come upon us—all of this is a part of not being perfect as our Lord and Savior is and because of the mystery of iniquity. Those who escape childhood and teenage years without any "scars" usually end up with some "war wounds" as adults for example through marital issues, drug, alcohol, and sex addictions."

"Teach, preacher," Mother Helen shouted out.

Kamal continued further, "Effects of the "damage" inflicted upon and by us produces some but not limited to low self-esteem, anger, fear, and ultimately isolation from people—not to have to deal with the aforementioned. Psalms 34:18 says, "The LORD is nigh unto them that are of a broken heart; and saveth such as be of a contrite spirit." When you look up the word "salvage," as a verb it means, "to collect or rescue an item; to save from harm or ruin."

"Come on, preacher!" Another person shouted out. Ondrea was enjoying the message and the service thus far.

"Right when we feel we are at that breaking point, His strength is then made perfect in our weakness and he saves us and delivers us from ourselves and that mental anguish and torment from the damage that has been done to us. He saves us through miracles and deliverance, in addition to using others to restore and encourage us to continue along this journey called life."

77

Thank You, Jesus! Ondrea closed her eyes and began to think back over her life, and all that God had done for her. She instantly felt joy. "Hallelujah," she shouted out. Alarmed, but feeling good at the same time, Ondrea knew she was free to praise God and happy to feel comfortable enough to.

"Alright now, I feel my help coming on!" Kamal exclaimed as he closed his Bible. "The definition of "purpose" means "the reason for which something is done or created for; for which something exists." Again, whether we were victims or caused certain things to befall our bodies and our lives, God still suffered it to be so that in our dark times and despair, we may know Him and His purpose.

You see, we cannot be born in and be of this world and fulfill God's purpose. God has to suffer us to some situations and circumstances for the usefulness and normal function that we would be equipped for in this world dies out, and that His Spirit can be resurrected and begin living in us. This is when we now have the value and normal function needed to operate in His Kingdom or "the Church." Remember saints that our life's story is but a mere chapter in someone else's book—let alone the only Bible they may ever read. We must let our light so shine so that God can get the glory! We do this by operating in the power of the Kingdom of God or the Church."

"Yes sir!" a young woman holding a baby yelled out.

"The meaning of "Damaged Goods" means, "a person regarded as inadequate or impaired in some way." Ministry occurs right here in the pulpit, in the streets, our schools, anyplace that we can be a vessel and allow God to use us to salvage others who have been damaged and have yet to realize the purpose of their pain. Those who are "impaired" and stuck in their mess, we are to remember that we once where they are…unable to move spiritually, emotionally, physically, mentally…never forget!"

"Teach, Minister!" Mother Helen stood up, clapping her hands in approval.

"Instead of forgetting or leaving them behind, or treating them as if they have leprosy or as the woman with the issue of blood and not come around or be in fellowship with us, we are to be strong and powerful enough that we shift the atmosphere that is controlling them. Our testimony and presence—if God truly resides within—is enough to command anyone's attention—no matter how deep in despair they may be. If you ever feel that you are inadequate to complete the task, you have to know that you didn't choose the calling, the calling chose you…Nobody gets the oil for what God called them to do without the crushing…everything you went through chose you because of the assignment, that's why He suffered it to be so! Romans 8:30 declares, "…And those God predestined, He also called; those He called, He also justified; those He justified, He also glorified!"

Ondrea felt herself getting up from the pew herself and standing up and joining Mother Helen, along with about half the congregation who were now all on their feet and praising God.

Kamal began to close out his message. "God has always been right there through the crushing and salvaged us all for such a time as now. His purpose for us to be an example of the REAL church of God—those of us who He has called out from the world into His Kingdom and trying to accomplish what thus says the Lord. Philippians 1:6 says, "Being confident of this very thing, that he which hath begun a good work in you will perform it until the day of Jesus Christ."

Ondrea looked around the room as various people began to shout and run around the Sanctuary as the Spirit fell in the service.

"Come hell or high water, nothing and no one can prevail against the Saints of God and the work that He has predestined for us to accomplish!"

That was it…Ondrea began to shout without restraint, and the entire congregation—including Minister Kamal went crazy and praised God for pouring out His Spirit on His people.

79

******

"I wish I would've brought my change of clothes in here with me," joked Mother Helen after service was over. Mostly everyone had cleared the Sanctuary, so at Mother Helen's discretion, she would escort Ondrea in the back where Minister Kamal's office was.

"Minister Davis already had Bryan bring your bags back here in his study for you to change or do what you needed to do after the service. There's a shower in there and I'll be here to stand guard…trust!" exclaimed Mother Helen.

This brotha is something serious…anointed, fine, thoughtful, and disciplined? Too good to be true… Ondrea finished her shower and got cute and comfy again in her pink Tom Ford hooded cashmere-blend dress and matching sneakers. She then said her goodbyes to Mother Helen and gathered her composure before Bryan escorted her back outside to Kamal's Cadillac.

*****

Kamal was eagerly awaiting Ondrea's arrival back into his car so he could finish his conversation with her. Again, he had prayed before she got inside his car, so he would stay strong. She was so beautiful to him… "pretty in pink." As she walked out of the church and towards his car, he tried his hardest not to study the switch in her hips as well as the chocolate thunder thighs she had exposed with each stride. *Lord, help me. I cannot take my eyes off of her. Patience and temperance, brotha,* he scolded himself. Kamal opened the car door for Ondrea, as she thanked Bryan for walking her to the car.

"So, this is how you operate, Minister Kamal?" she asked.

"What you mean, Ms. Lady?" he replied, biting his lower lip and winked.

Instantly, Ondrea felt her body getting warm on the inside. She began to blush, "the hotel, being so attentive and thoughtful, delivering the Word with power the way you do...practically spoiling me this weekend?"

"Straight like that," he replied coolly. "Let's talk about how you operate..."

"Whatever do you mean, Minister?"

"Say you don't know about being baptized, but mess around and have the Spirit take over you and shout all over my church."

"Whatever, man!" Ondrea playfully shoved him in the arm.

"What did I tell you about messing with a man while he's driving...don't make me pull this car over, Ms. Lady..."

"And what?" Ondrea continued playfully. "The only time you better pull this car over is if you're stopping for us to grab something to eat."

Kamal's tone switched to more serious, "My apologies, I just started driving, and didn't even consider if you were hungry..."

"I didn't mean it in that way," Ondrea stated cutting him off, "I could eat though...nothing fancy, just some soul food."

"Now, that I can get with," he agreed.

*****

They had decided to dine in, and this again was the perfect time for him to finish yesterday's conversation. Kamal pulled up at Frank's Cajun & Soul Kitchen due to the two-hour wait at Chef Vino's

81

restaurant. The waiter took their drink orders and Kamal got straight to the point as soon as they left the table to put the order in for their food.

"So, yesterday, you left off on how you felt God covered and protected you in every area except for one…please, continue that for me."

Ondrea gave Kamal a look, however, it was her idea first to play this game…

"He never shielded me from the hurt and pain I felt after my first love…"

Ondrea's voice trailed off as she looked away from Kamal and out of the window. *I can do this. I got this…stay strong.* Ondrea gassed herself up to finish… "I met him on my last day of high school when I was turning eighteen. He was twenty years old at the time, but we had a vibe and real strong connection, you know."

"I see…keep going, lady," Kamal replied.

Ondrea took a deep breath, "you ain't right, Minister," she retorted playfully.

Kamal reached across the table to grab her hand for reassurance and support, "This was your idea, to begin with, now come on with it," he replied.

"He was my first everything…first love, the first person I had ever had sex with my husband and the father of my daughter." Ondrea started to wipe away the tears from her face. "He was getting himself together, you know…he didn't tell me he sold drugs until after I had already fallen for him, and the rest is history."

"So, whatever happened to him? Are you two still married?" *That makes sense*, Kamal reasoned…*that is why she said it was complicated.*

More tears began to fall as she brought herself to say the words, "He was killed before he even had a chance to see his daughter be born…they took him away from me."

It was at that moment that Kamal wanted to always protect, honor, love, and cherish Ondrea. Such a beautiful woman and soul that had been crushed by her first heartbreak, and all the remnants of the broken picture shattered in her heart and not to mention the heart of her daughter—who had to grow up, like him too—knowing she would never have the opportunity to have her father, let alone even know who he was besides what someone else told her.

"You and your daughter must be super close though now because of all you two have had to go through since his death…I'm so sorry you have had to experience this, but if you can hold onto anything that you can from my message on this morning…there's a purpose to your pain, lady."

"Yes, my daughter and I are close…We're all we have. I'm so proud of the young lady she is becoming…she'll be sixteen in February, and she wants this big elaborate party at a skating rink here…because she's also an honor student and so accomplished with school and cheer, I almost feel obligated to give her what she wants because she doesn't cause me any grief."

"Then throw her the party, you only turn sixteen once."

"You sound like her now," Ondrea chuckled.

The waiter came back with their food, and Ondrea realized as they were eating that Kamal had not answered the question in return.

"Wait a minute, Mr.!" she exclaimed. "You know you have to answer the question also…"

"I didn't have that experience," he stated.

"So, you've never been hurt in life outside of your parents? Family member? Anyone? I don't believe that…"

83

Kamal looked Ondrea dead in her eyes with a look so intense, and stated, "I never put myself in a position to be hurt after leaving home."

"So that explains why you have no children and had multiple women…I get it."

"Growing up the way that I did and seeing some things no kid really should ever have to see, it left my vision so blurry, I thought wrong was right, and vice versus. Our motto back in 'the life,' was literally 'F everything and everybody, get you one or two bad chicks, and get this money."

"That's a big transformation from that mindset, to now being a preacher."

"Tell me about it…the most serious decision that I have ever had to make in my life, and I do not regret it for one second."

The waiter cleared their plates, and Kamal paid for their bill. The two of them got back in the car and braced themselves for the car ride for the next 3 hours.

Kamal decided to keep the old school game going, but with a twist. "Ondrea, I'm switching this game up a little."

"What do you have in mind, then?"

"You got me going back to my childhood days with the questions, so might as well do Truth or Dare."

"Alright, you're taking it back…"

"Truth or Dare?" Kamal asked.

"Truth."

"Ondrea, have you ever tried to date anyone else after your late husband?"

Ondrea thought to herself for a second, and suddenly a huge smile spread across her face. "There was this one guy who tried to talk to me, and I thought maybe possibly it was going to go somewhere, but then I realized he was a hoe, so it would never work out…"

"A hoe now?" Kamal belted out a hearty laugh. "Hey, go easy on a brother, I got all that out my system, trust."

"Who said I was talking about you, Minister…careful, you're telling on yourself?"

"Oh, shoot…" Kamal returned with the embarrassment in his tone. "But then again, I told you the old mindset I used to have…"

Ondrea could not hold her joke any longer, and burst out laughing, "I'm just playing."

Kamal shot her a dirty look and turned his eyes back on the road.

"Aww…did I hurt your feelings?" Ondrea took Kamal's hand in hers and held it before he jerked his away from hers. "I said I apologized, geesh!"

He flashed his pearly whites as he turned towards her laughing again. "Gotcha!" He took her hand back into his, and they kept their hands intertwined.

"No, but to be serious, I tried to move past him, but any guy that I met—we couldn't get past thirty days."

"Seriously? Well then should I feel special since it has been about three months for us talking?"

Ondrea smiled, "yeah, this is really an unordinary dating story so far…but anyways, my turn…So truth or dare?

"Dare."

"What, Minister…you wanna take a walk on the 'Wild Side'?" Ondrea was shocked.

Kamal remained silent.

"Okay, I dare you to take a selfie with me and then send it to my phone."

"You aren't gonna photoshop me and have me in some kind of preacher's scandal, are you?" he asked.

"No sir, God looking at me…" she answered in a serious manner.

"Alright," he obliged and took a selfie with Ondrea. Her touch was so gentle when she put her arm around him while they had stopped at the stop light. He then sent the pic to her. *Perfect look. We look good together.*

"So, it's back on me now…"

"Truth," Ondrea replied.

"Have you ever thought about being a First lady?"

"I never thought I'd be in this position or dating a man like you. I mostly attracted the bad guys…don't know what that is necessarily."

"But aren't you the psychologist, here?"

"Everyone knows that every therapist has their own personal therapist," she said jokingly.

"Well, most people who bring healing usually attract the wounded or broken," Kamal answered matter-of-factly.

He was turning her on with his conversation. The fact that she met someone who intellectually could stimulate her mind had her questioning what about her he liked since she was broken herself.

86

"Why do you find me attractive?" Ondrea asked.

"That's too easy...you're corny..."

"Excuse me!" Ondrea replied while huffing and crossing her arms with disgust.

"Don't get offended, lady...the fact that you have a grown man out here playing these childhood classic games...and laughing and enjoying myself doing it is a compliment."

"I guess you can continue then," she replied.

"Also, the fact that you're a naturally beautiful woman...that is extremely hard to come by. You got fake breasts, butts, lashes, lace fronts, bundles, contacts...you name it (in my Shirley Ceaser voice)," he joked. "But on the real—you have pretty feet, you don't have to wear any makeup and still killing 'em..."

He paused and looked her directly in her eyes with a stare so intense she had to look away momentarily.

"Look at me, Ondrea..."

She reluctantly turned her face back towards him. She was blushing with embarrassment. Again, she hadn't felt this way since she was with Chance.

"The fact that you take pride in your appearance and they way you dress...your conversation, I also love. The fact that we can pull things out of each other that we may not have shared with anyone else other than God is a huge turn on for me. Your sexy, and you know it."

They didn't realize that with all the questions and conversation, they had already gotten to their destination. Kamal pulled into Dearron and Bria's driveway. He stared at Ondrea and smiled. Her heart did safely trust him, and he could feel it. He could not believe he found a woman that possessed all the unselfish qualities his mother never had...or any woman for that matter.

Kamal got out and followed behind her with her bags.

"Hold up," Ondrea said mid-stride up the path to their front door. "You can just put my bags in the trunk of my car while it's parked outside…"

"Gotcha, I'm a secret," Kamal added.

"Not really, I just don't want my daughter to meet you like this."

"Oh, so I get to meet the fam now?" he grinned.

He's so fine…stay focused, 'Drea. She reached out to hug him.

Kamal did not think before leaning in to hug her. She smelled so good, and her body felt good cozied up on his. She pulled back from their embrace so she could look him in the eyes.

"I enjoyed my weekend, Kamal…"

"What?! No formalities this time?! I'm shocked!" he teased.

"You earned it," she sang playfully in her best interpretation of The Weekend's hit song as she leaned back in to hug him again. She then kissed him on the cheek and stepped back out of the embrace.

Kamal was not prepared for this moment and was now at a loss for words. Although he wanted to return the favor, he kissed her on the top of her forehead and stepped back from her so that he was not further tempted to do something he would regret later. As soon as she stepped inside her friend's home, Kamal immediately started to go into prayer mode. His foot almost slipped tonight, and he still wanted to court her the right way—timing is everything.

Once he had backed out of the driveway, he pulled his phone out to text Ondrea: **"I enjoyed your company, Ms. Lady…a little too much. Lol. Glad we stopped when we did. I can't kiss someone I'm not courting (smile).**

Chapter Fourteen

Ondrea was not all the way even in the guest bedroom when Bria stepped out into the hallway after checking on Jonoah and pushing her through the doorway to get details.

"Cow, Tania ended up spending the night last night with Dane, since Treasure came to visit him this weekend and 'D left about fifteen minutes ago to pick her up."

"Thanks again, cow," Ondrea replied knowing Treasure and Tania got along and are about the same age. Dane (Dearron's twin) and Treasure's mother were not together anymore, so it wasn't that often they were able to spend time together whenever Tania and Ondrea came down to visit due to visitation arrangements.

"So, spill it!" Bria urged.

Ondrea exhaled slowly, "I have to thank you and 'D for introducing us…he is beyond amazing, friend. He's so thoughtful and showed he could be very protective of me if I did give him a chance…"

"Did you spend the night with him? Was he on his best behavior?" Bria squealed with curiosity.

"He had a room waiting for me at The Four Seasons hotel and paid for spa treatments in advance for me…he didn't even try to come in!"

"Now that's what I'm talking about! A brotha that's saved, sexy and spending…"

"Bria, you always have to go over the top," Ondrea added playfully.

"Well, you're welcome, cow…oh, how was his church? I know you enjoyed his preaching because you have to be wearing a seatbelt when it comes to staying in your seat while he's bringing the Word."

"His message was right on time, and you're right…I ended up shouting for the first time."

"Gone 'head, girl!" Bria replied with excitement.

"I know…I feel like that song Kierra Sheard sings, 'It Keeps Happening for Me'…when I let go of so many fears, nothing but joy has come my way. It's almost scary in the same breath."

"And that can happen…are you going to start attending church there now?"

"I think I just might. He asked me if I wanted to get baptized, and I told him I wasn't ready for all of that…. I even want to do that now."

"Ummm hmmm…and which kind of baptism are you talking about?" Bria said jokingly.

"Really, cow!" Ondrea shrieked. "Both—sike, I'm just playing…although our chemistry is becoming too much. I kissed him, and he was looking at me like he was gonna tongue me. down but stepped away from me. He's so disciplined, and my emotions were all over the place…I really can't believe I let my guard all the way down with him."

"Then you better marry that Man of God when he asks—not if—when. He looks like he is nobody that plays around in those sheets, and he's solid 'Drea! There is no dirt anyone can find on him—not one scandal with any women, and with no kids, means no baggage, girl!"

"One of the Mothers at his church that he had me sit with told me the same thing. She said that he hasn't come to her to discuss any women in a while…"

"That's because your mourning is now being turned into dancing. This opportunity for love doesn't happen just any random time…God did that, cow!"

"Even if you're right about all of this, I still need to know that Tania would be okay with me dating him and possibly marrying him at some point."

"Girl, Tania will be grown and out of your house in 3 more years…you better live your life for yourself. Watch everything fall into place as it has been anyway. You know the opportunity for her to have a father-figure—especially right now in her life can't hurt any more than it would help."

The two heard the garage opening and decided to wrap up their conversation and head downstairs before 'D and Tania came into the house.

"Hey, God mommy…hey Mom," Tania sang out as she entered the living room. "What did I miss while I was gone?" Tania knew something was up, especially whenever her mother is okay with her not being in her sight overnight.

"Nothing, Honey. I was just filling Bria in here about a church that I attended today and enjoyed the service and wanted to keep visiting to see how the worship there goes."

"That is cool, Mom. What is the name of the church? I might want to go with you instead of Londyn next time."

Even though Ondrea never went to church after Chance died, Ondrea never wanted her thoughts and experiences to cloud the judgment and faith of her daughter. Over the years, whenever Tania asked to spend the night on Saturdays and go to church with her friends and their families, she never stepped in between it.

It's called Destiny to Faith Deliverance Ministries…"

"…No way, Mom!" Tania exclaimed. "That is where Londyn and her parents go to church…I have been going there…" Tania then turned to Bria, "and tried to get my mom to come with me and worship there for forever!"

"That's awesome news to hear, Taniecey-pooh," replied Bria.

"I have to go tell God daddy the news...and Londyn, I so geeked!" said Tania, as she ran back down the hallway to find 'D and let him in on the wonderful news.

Both Ondrea and Bria looked at each other in surprise. Ondrea knew she had seen the name of his church somewhere—the first time Tania came home excited about her visit there with Londyn's family and gave her the Sunday bulletin to look over. This was awesome news.

"See cow," Bria clasped her hands together in praise, "That means Tania was already familiar with Kamal, and hopefully the transition from preacher to possible stepfather might not prove to be so difficult after all. Remember what I said, everything will fall in line."

The two of them hugged, and Ondrea went to say her goodbyes to 'D and checked her phone while waiting on Tania to bring her things to the car. She could not help but smile when she read the text from Kamal.

"Well, I guess we're courting now, lol" she replied flirtatiously, **"Have a good night, Kamal. I cannot wait until our time to talk tomorrow...let me know when you make it back safe. My daughter and I are leaving now, and I have a surprise to tell you when we talk. Have a good night, Minister (smile).**

Chapter Fifteen

"Can you believe Homecoming is this weekend?" asked Londyn as she and Tania had finished changing out of their school clothes and into their workout clothes for cheer practice.

"I know, right!" Tania exclaimed. "Is everything still a go for Friday?" she asked.

"Of course. My parents are going to be at the Mint Condition concert, and my mom was telling my Aunt Sandy that my dad got them a room somewhere to spend time afterward since it's your weekend your over at our house…something about their privacy."

"Ewww," stated Tania. "But that means we'll have the house to ourselves afterward?"

"At least until the early morning…if we had Sebastian and T over, they would need to be gone by the morning…unless, we go someplace with them, and just make sure we're back home by the morning…"

A wide grin spread across Tania's face. She loved when Londyn thought up her great schemes. They had been able to link up with Sebastian and her cousin many times on the weekends and had become addicted to spending time more and more with their boyfriends. After Sebastian had told her that he thought he might be falling in love with her, Tania knew she would never break up with him. She loved when they would make out with each other, he would buy her little trinkets here and there, or just spending time falling asleep on the phone with each other. She had sent him a couple of suggestive pictures here and there over the last month, but nothing further than third base.

Sebastian watched Tania and her girl walk out of the girl's locker room. He knew that he was a lucky guy to have Tania Williams as his girl, *but what good was it to have the keys to a Maybach, but not be able to drive it?* Although being patient was one of his strongest qualities, Sebastian was starting to become frustrated with her "teasing," as he called it. He was not a virgin like she was, and he tried to remember that, but he was sixteen, and his hormones were raging. He knew there were other girls interested in him, and had even tried to throw some at him, but he cared about Tania deeply—even believed he loved her…and he did not want to play her. Plus, he knew that her cousin 'T would have him beat senseless if he found out that Sebastian played his cousin.

"Don't drool so hard, player," 'T said playfully as he walked up behind him.

"Aw, naw I was just admiring my view."

"Yeah, I see all that, just don't enjoy the view too much, if you know what I mean."

"Dude, you and Londyn been smashing for the past week!" retorted Sebastian annoyed.

"Don't hate on us, player," 'T stated. "Londyn damn sure ain't my cousin, and unfortunately for you homie, Tania is."

"But you ain't trying to wife Londyn or stay with her like I want to with Tania…"

"You don't know what I'm trying to do with what I and Londyn got going on…"

"So…She got to you, huh?"

"Got to me ain't even the word…man, she put it on me in the worst way, and it's the mental that's getting to me."

95

"For real?"

"Yeah, it's that deep with her. I mean, she's in that physics track, so already she turns me on with her brain that way…the other stuff is cool too though, don't get it twisted…I love it when she throw it back on a player!"

"Dude, you are retarded!" Sebastian laughed.

"Naw, I'm working on making her mine the long way…maybe we can be like my cousin's parents were when they met."

"What? You for real?"

"Yeah cuz, straight up nobody can say or do anything to make me ever leave that girl," he stated waving at her to come over as she exited the locker room.

Both she and Tania made their way over to both boys and greeted them with hugs. 'T grabbed Londyn's butt, while Sebastian carefully palmed Tania's firmly while they hugged the girls back.

"So, we were hoping you guys are still able to hook up with us after the homecoming game this Friday…Tania is spending the night with me, so we'll already be together to link."

'T's eyes lit up, "my dad is taking some chick to that Mint Condition concert, so I'm good this way, love…ya'll can come chill at the house, and I can take one of Pop's whips and drop ya'll off when you're ready to go home."

Sebastian was nervous about asking his parents to spend the night at Tyrin's. His parents already weren't too fond of 'T, or the fact that his father was a felon. He was going to have to try something though. He did not get too many opportunities to spend extended time with Tania. He thought he might even be able to get lucky this time.

"I'll figure something out, but I'm down," added Sebastian.

Ms. Grace's Tesla pulled up on time, and the girls said their goodbyes and got inside the car—super excited and anticipating Friday's events.

Chapter Sixteen

Ondrea and Kamal could not stop texting back and forth with each other all week. Ondrea kept looking at the time, counting down to when she would be able to tell him her surprise news about meeting Tania and joining his church. She also had won some Mint Condition tickets at work, and since she kissed him, she wanted to make sure if he would still consider being her date. *I have a boyfriend...who wants to eventually marry me...all of this in a matter of two months...this is crazy!*

The difference this time around is that they had talked over the phone and face times, getting to know each other first before meeting again in person. They had established a mental connection first before anything, and that was more powerful than anything sexual.

After she decided to agree to him courting her, she felt an intense need to be around him and see him. Kamal told her that he did not think that it would be a good idea and that they needed to just keep their interactions to the phone because he wanted to make sure he did right by her and God—stating that it would be his job to present his bride spotless and blameless on her wedding day.

Little did he know, the more he tried to be respectful of her body and feelings in their talks in addition to his actions with daily conversation and random gifts and flowers being delivered to her every day at work—Kamal was turning Ondrea on even the more. Whatever he may have been feeling, even with praying, he felt the weakest he had ever had in years. All he knew was that just the sight of her every time they Face timed, or the sound of her voice had him feeling things that he had never felt with any other woman. He knew it was not lusting either, but the desire to connect with the woman he had already made up in his mind that he was going to marry. He looked at the clock, prayed, and began to contact her.

Ondrea was wearing her Balmain pinstripe jumpsuit, with her hair down. Her phone rang.

"Hey beautiful," Kamal stated as Ondrea watched him walk up and down his balcony. He was dressed in a blue Nike tracksuit.

"Hey handsome, you look nice," she replied. "I miss you."

"I miss you too, lady."

"So how did your last meeting turn out?" Ondrea asked in concern.

Kamal had told her about Bryan and some of the other deacons at the church who wanted the other pastor to step down and have him take the position as Senior Pastor of the church.

"Well, it got pretty heated, and I had to help intervene when Bryan and Pastor Thomas was about to fight. I hadn't fought anyone, let alone been in that kind of setting in a long time…just threw me off."

"I'm so sorry that you had to be pulled in that arena. I have an idea to help bring you back to some peace and some tranquility…"

"Okay woman, what do you have in mind?"

"Well, tomorrow is the Mint Condition concert at Mable House Barnes Amphitheater, and I know I mentioned it before to you, but I want to make sure you can come…it would be a good stress reliever for you—not to mention I would like to spend some time with my man…it feels good to even say those words."

Kamal hesitantly agreed to go and stated that he would pick her up about an hour before the concert was to start.

"Well, I wanted to surprise you and let you know tomorrow is also my daughter's homecoming game, and I'd like for you to come a little earlier to help me see her off."

"Wow, that is quite the surprise. I know she means the world to you…I feel honored and blessed to do so."

Ondrea's smile became even wider. She was so excited and figured she would wait until tomorrow to share the other surprise with him.

"Thanks so much, babe!" she exclaimed while jumping up and down.

Kamal was happy to be able to put that big of a smile on Ondrea's face. He was now smiling as well just thinking about how everything was lining up the way that it was supposed to. After deciding on a final time for him to show up at her place and saying their goodbyes over the phone, Kamal prayed again, thanking God for the strength to stay in control of his emotions and feelings. He then decided to go on a fast-starting from 6 am to 6 pm tomorrow to help maintain his strength. He knew she was his weakness and would need it, especially after she just asked him to meet her daughter. Everything from this moment forward seemed so final and official. He knew he needed to contact 'D and see if Bria would talk with him in regard to setting up a surprise engagement to Ondrea, and also help with making sure he picked out the right ring for her.

Chapter Seventeen

Tania stood in the mirror smiling at the results. Her homecoming outfit, along with accessories and hair did up in a pony twist…she knew tonight would be the bomb.com with Sebastian. He had told her earlier at school that he had bought some condoms just in case she was ready tonight. Somehow, Tania could not get the conversation with her mother out of her head about having sex. She wanted to honor God, her mother, and her body, but she loved Sebastian and wanted to make sure that he never has a chance to doubt it.

When the doorbell rang, Tania flew down the stairs to answer it, thinking it was Londyn, however it was Minister Kamal Davis, the Associate Pastor, and her Sunday School teacher.

"Hi, Minister Davis…" Tania started with confusion. "What are you doing here at my house?"

"Wow, I had no idea Ondrea is your mother!" he exclaimed, hugging her.

"Surprise to the both of you," Ondrea said with excitement as she snuck up on both.

"Mom, you're dating?! And Minister Davis?"

"I'm sorry for you to find out this way, Tania…I understand if…" Kamal started.

"No, I'm so happy about this, you guys!" Tania squealed with delight. "How cool is it to know my mom is dating a preacher? So that's why you came to the church finally…I've been trying for the past year to get her to come with me…"

"Well, not entirely true, Tania. God has been dealing with me in a very real way, and Kamal has been the one supporting me on this journey step-by-step. It started that way but very recently has turned into something more. I've decided to join your ministry, meaning my daughter and I should be active members in your church effective this Sunday."

"God is good," said Kamal in appreciation. "I'm so happy to hear this, Ondrea…and it's good to know that you approve of me courting your mother."

"Please keep working on my mom, I'm loving everything I'm hearing right now," Tania said jokingly. "If you two will excuse me, I'm gonna finish getting ready before Londyn comes to pick me up… See you on Sunday, Minister Davis."

"You look fine already," Ondrea replied.

"Mom, you would say that…" she stated as she left to return upstairs.

"Teenagers," Ondrea replied as she rolled her eyes and turned her attention back to Kamal. "This age is a challenge."

"Well, I'll be here to help in any way I can. You won't have to do anything alone with me."

"This is like a fairytale dream come true," Ondrea stated as she hugged Kamal. The doorbell rang again.

"Tania, it's Londyn!" Ondrea called out.

Tania said final goodbyes to both her mom and Kamal and then left with her overnight bag. She was ready for the night's festivities to begin.

"Ondrea, I'm waiting…we're gonna be late," Kamal called out to her upstairs. He wished that she would hurry up and finish getting ready. He did not want to start getting comfortable in her home…he was prayed up and trying to keep it that way.

"Coming, babe!" Ondrea replied as she kept staring in the mirror. Even though Kamal kept it casual when he popped up at her home for the evening in black jeans, a simple black and yellow cardigan sweater with yellow Distinct Life "Inspire" Pumas, she still wanted to match his fly—even when he called himself dressing down for a change. By 6:50 pm, she was seductively cute in some black leggings with a denim irregular hem dress, and matching Tory Burch sneakers.

Chapter Eighteen

"Aye, ya'll, keep it down in there!" Tania yelled at both her cousin and her best friend who appeared to be getting it on in his bedroom.

"Don't hate on them, slim," said Sebastian as he tried to plant a kiss on Tania's lips as they were laying down on the couch at 'T's. He was excited, and on top of their school winning their game, he wanted to "score" with her as well.

Tania pulled away slowly when Sebastian's hands started sliding down towards her private area. She became very uneasy and knew right then and there that this was not going to be the night it went down.

"Sebastian, don't."

"Man, I knew this was gonna happen!" He lamented.

"What do you mean by that?" Tania asked demandingly.

Sebastian knew he had crossed the line with her. "I'm just saying, I didn't know that you still were having second thoughts again…"

"I didn't know either, Sebastian…you act like I don't want to make this happen between us."

"I don't know, slim…I'm starting to think something different."

Tania reached out and grabbed both of his hands, "Come on baby, don't be like this."

"Listening to your cousin and Londyn getting it in is not how I imagined our first homecoming together to be."

"At least we're the only freshman…we have at least three more homecomings to attend together"

"I hear you, babe. But I will be honest, I don't know if I can wait that long."

"So, what are you suggesting then?"

"I mean, I love and care about you deeply, but I also want to be with someone who wants the same as I do—I'm not saying that you don't love me or anything, but I want to be with someone who is not afraid and comfortable with me enough to express that."

"But I have done that Sebastian… I even have sent pictures of my body to you and you say something like this to me?!"

"I only want to be honest with you, babe. I love you."

"No, you don't, because if you did you wouldn't pressure me to have sex with you…you'd be more understanding of how I feel because I am still a virgin…you would be patient and kind towards me—not having the crappy attitude that you are having right now."

"That is from blue balls, Tania…you don't understand everything that I have to do to myself whenever I leave from being with you. I am always backed up…I am needing to release with you…. who else am I supposed to release my all to, but my girl?"

You could try God, you know! Tania thought to herself. She was heated with anger at this moment. She could not believe how ridiculous her boyfriend was acting towards her, not to mention the fact that she thought about giving it up to him tonight only to find him treating her this way all because she had morals and standards set for herself. Ondrea got up from the couch and ran into the bathroom to cry while Sebastian popped in the movie, Got My Hustle Up.

Tania was so glad that she had listened to her mother. *Thank You God for covering me, even when I wanted to do wrong,* she prayed to herself as she waited for 'T and Londyn to finish so that they could hurry and get back to Londyn's house.

Chapter Nineteen

As per usual, Mint Condition delivered with the live band's groovy sounds, with Stokely killing the vocals even better than when the group first came out. They performed all their greatest hits, and even both Kamal and Ondrea enjoyed the opening act from spoken word artist, iWitness Life. As they were heading out of the amphitheater, Ondrea spotted Londyn's parents.

"Please don't call them over…I don't want anything to be awkward about this night," Kamal stated. "It took me some time to agree to this because of me being a minister. It's crazy always having to second-guess activities, concerts, different outings all because of one wrong move, and I'll kill my testimony, my name, and possibly our church's reputation for being a powerful and spirit-filled ministry."

"That sounds like a lot of pressure…almost the pressure to be perfect."

"Listen to you preaching already, Evangelist," he added jokingly. "God never called us to be perfect, but He called us to be Holy."

"True," Ondrea replied in agreement.

They were almost to the front door when Ondrea bumped into a man in passing—*hold up…* "Tyrin?!" she asked with a shocked look on her face. "You're here with Taylor?! How do you two know each other?"

Taylor put her head down as Tyrin began to explain. "What's up cousin, I knew Taylor from around the way back in the day. Her hubby is away on business, so she's tending to her business with me," he added as he put his arms around her waist.

"So, you're cool with that, 'Rin?" Ondrea asked as she eyed Taylor while shaking her head.

"T and I go way back, 'Drea. Her dude ain't as legit as he put out either, so I say it's payback he deserves—and really I could've had him handled if she gave me that green light…who's dude?" he asked Ondrea while staring Kamal up and down with a scowl.

"I'm Kamal Davis, Ondrea's boyfriend," Kamal extended his hand.

Tyrin chose not to return the gesture, "do I know you from somewhere?" he asked Kamal instead.

"I can't call it, but you do look familiar also…"

"What's your street name?"

"I'm not in "the life" anymore, bro."

"He's a preacher, 'Rin!" Ondrea rushed in. Kamal shot her a look.

"Alright, that's what's up," Tyrin replied. "Later 'Drea," he said as he grabbed Taylor by the waist and escorted her outside and to his car.

"Bye, 'Rin…Taylor," Ondrea replied.

"Bye, Ondrea," Taylor returned.

"Don't mind him, babe…" Ondrea assured Kamal. "…he's just salty because I called him out on committing adultery with my friend's homegirl, on top of finally seeing that I've moved on from Chance."

"Who is Chance, babe?!"

"He was my husband. Tyrin was Chance's cousin, so he's been a part of our family since we had met, and more so after Chance died."

"It's cool, babe," Kamal stated. "I'm gonna get the car and bring it around. *So, he probably just wanted to test me to see if I measured up to his cousin? I am not that person anymore,* Kamal reminded himself. *Old things are passed away and behold all things become new…strongholds no longer control me. Whatever this feeling is in me, Lord please take it away as soon as it came. I will enjoy my time with my lady, and I thank and praise You in advance, Amen.*

*****

It took Kamal and Ondrea over forty-five minutes to arrive at her house with the traffic. The ride back had been filled with awkward silence, and Ondrea did not want to end the night like this.

"Babe, I apologize for him offending you, but please don't let that encounter ruin our night."

"You're right, lady," Kamal snapped back to himself. "My apologies, babe…and it's getting late…"

"You might as well come inside and stay for a little while…you owe me." She added while giving him puppy dog eyes.

"Not those eyes, lady…do not do me like that…alright, but just for a little while. I still have to head back home."

"You can just stay here…I have a guest bedroom…just rest and you can head out after I make some breakfast for you in the morning. No pressure, I promise."

109

Again, Kamal was not prepared for if he had to stay around Ondrea in a space where it was just the two of them. *Lord, help me,* he prayed before heading inside.

Ondrea showed him the guest suite in the basement. Kamal was impressed with her welcome basket that made him already feel right at home. She had the basket filled with Perrier water, peppermints, toothbrush, Dove unscented soap, mouthwash, towel, and a washcloth. *How hospitable,* he thought. He heard the bath water running in the bathroom, and instantly got nervous. *I should go ahead and leave…this is not a good set up.*

Ondrea sensed that Kamal might be uneasy, so she made sure she informed him of what she was doing. "Don't worry, I'm running this for you to take. I'll be upstairs, but I want to make sure that you get taken care of…you always are having to care for others at your church, you looked out for me this weekend, and I just wanted you to be able to wind down from the drama from earlier—as well as show my appreciation for you."

Kamal nodded his head in approval. No one had ever considered his feelings before, and he was shocked beyond words at Ondrea's gesture. "Thank you so much for this…I really don't know what to say." The wonderful scent of lavender filled the entire room, "What all did you put in my bathwater; I love the scent coming from the bathroom."

"It's Lavender oil from Cream Blends—I swear by their products…Just enjoy your bath and I will see you in the morning, preacher," Ondrea blew a kiss at him as she closed the door behind her and headed back upstairs.

I cannot believe this woman is real, Kamal thought to himself while in the bathtub. *Thank You, Lord* was all he said as he closed his eyes and soaked all his stresses away.

*****

Kamal opened his eyes the next morning around 10:00 am. *I can't believe I slept in this long...I must have needed this kind of rest.* He saw that there was a text from Ondrea instructing him to open the door for a surprise. Once he opened the door, there inside of a Nordstrom's bag, was a black Nike tracksuit, white tee shirt and even matching socks and underwear for him to put on. *She is A-1 alright,* he smiled as he took the clothes out to prepare to put on and head upstairs. The wonderful smell of bacon, eggs, smoked sausage, grits, and pancakes filled the kitchen as he entered.

"Good morning, sleepyhead!" Ondrea exclaimed.

"Good morning, beautiful...so, this is what we're doing now?"

"Indeed, Mr. Davis...I didn't have much time to hurry to the store to get the things I wanted you to have, but they did the job I see...make sure you eat up, sir," Ondrea replied flirtatiously. She had set out both the orange juice and Sangria flavored juice cartons, along with water since she didn't know what he might want to drink.

Kamal laughed, "You play too much...you better be glad I'm prayed up right now," he stated biting his bottom lip.

"See, you can't be doing that to me!" Ondrea exclaimed. "That is a turn on for me when you bite your bottom lip."

"Okay, I'll try not to do it so much around you, until you're my Mrs," he replied.

After they finished eating their food, Kamal insisted on washing up the dishes. "I don't want to leave your place a mess," he added.

111

You can be as messy as you want…Stop it, 'Drea! she warned herself. She was completely turned on and wanted Kamal in the worst way. She could stop while she was ahead, but temptation had gotten the best of her. It had been four years since she had been with someone intimately, but the combination of knowing she was dating to marry, in addition to the strong mental and emotional chemistry she felt in his presence was overwhelmingly powerful beyond her ability to be patient.

Kamal entered the living room after he finished, only to find that Ondrea was already in her living room loading a movie for their viewing pleasure. "So, what's it gonna be…Brown Sugar or play some cards or Uno before you hit the road?"

"Let's watch the movie then," Kamal replied sitting down.

"Okay," she pressed play, walked over towards him to join him on the loveseat.

Kamal could not stop watching her hips as she came towards him. "This is gonna be a weird question, but do you think you can change your clothes?"

"Excuse me?!" Ondrea said, obviously bothered, "what's wrong with my clothes, Kamal? You were with me all night when I wore some leggings…"

"Yeah, out in public though. You got me here where I spent the night, and you in some more leggings walking around me…"

Ondrea couldn't take the tension anymore. She hurried to plant her lips onto Kamal's while he was mid-sentence. Kamal bit his bottom lip while staring at her seductively and returned the kiss. The two of them kissed so passionately and aggressively that her body began to get hot instantly, *this man does not play any games,* she thought to herself. "Kamal," she whispered in his ear, "what has gotten into you, babe." His hands began to pull her closer to him. She then straddled him on the couch, where they continued to make out. Right when she tried to unzip his tracksuit jacket, he suddenly pulled back.

"What am I doing?! Ondrea, I must apologize…I told you that I am trying to do right by you. You aren't my wife yet, and until then I don't want to start anything that we won't be able to stop."

"I don't want to stop, babe," Ondrea sighed in frustration, as she continued to try and kiss Kamal some more while he gently lifted her off him, and seating her down on the couch.

"Believe me, I don't want either," he said standing up.

"Don't leave right now," she replied, looking down at his print that was now bulging like crazy. "You don't want to try and watch the movie…"

"No, trust me... It's for the best…we both know we aren't gonna watch no movie Ondrea," Kamal said with a hearty laugh.

Ondrea nodded in agreement and got up to show him to the door, and his eyes stayed fixated on her leggings and backside. *Lord, please help me help myself.*

"Can I have another kiss before I leave you?"

"Kissing can lead to so many other things, lady…just look at us now—I am about ready to throw my whole salvation away and risk it all to have some of you," Kamal added as he gave her a loving embrace, squeezing her tightly.

She could feel Kamal through their clothing, and although her body was yearning for him to unleash all of who he was on and in her, she knew that he was right about keeping the reign on things until marriage. *I must help him stay strong...*

"I have to respect you, especially when you're respecting me, Kamal...You're right...you have to go."

"Bye, Ondrea...I'll call when I get in," he said as he watched her close the door. *Thank You Lord for making a way of escape in my temptation, I should have never come in, to begin with. I will do right by You, Lord, and Ondrea. In Jesus' name, I pray, Amen.*

*****

BRING!!!!

The phone rang, and Ondrea saw a number that she hadn't recognized. "Hello?"

"Hey..." Taylor's phone trailed off.

"What's up, Taylor? I was incredibly surprised to see what I saw..."

Taylor cut her off. "...Before you go judging someone, your cousin wasn't wrong about my husband...you don't even know what I deal with."

"I hear you, Taylor but I still don't understand why you don't just divorce him then...Tyrin is doing well now, so you could see what's up with you two...how long have you guys been messing around?"

"When he had first got out of jail…I wasn't even with Charles yet…I had taken my car to get some work done, and he was there…the rest is history. You know Tyrin though, he can't leave the women alone, so that's why we never worked out, 'Drea…we just stayed connected over the years, and whenever I need a shoulder to cry on, or an ear to listen, he makes everything alright…Mr. Feel Good is who Tyrin is for me."

"Wow…I'm so sorry that this has been your life, Taylor. I'm gonna pray that your situation gets better, but in the meantime, you should still think about divorcing him. Even if you and Tyrin never settle down together, at least you won't be committing adultery and stooping to the same level as Charles. You deserve better, sweetie."

"You're right, 'Drea…I guess I'm just nervous of what the congregation would think…you know that church is all I know."

"You could join ours, heffa!" Ondrea exclaimed.

"That is something to think about…I'm glad I talked to you, Ondrea."

"Me too, Taylor…have a good rest of the day girl."

As much as she wanted to call and tell Bria about what happened with Taylor, and her and Kamal, she thought *"some things are best kept to yourself."*

Chapter Twenty

After that night, things became difficult for Tania and Sebastian. He was trying his hardest to be patient, but again, with other girls interested in him his interest in Tania began to diminish. She knew that she had made the right decision, and everything else in her life continued to flourish.

Kamal had asked her back around Thanksgiving how she felt about him proposing to her mother during their Watch Night service on New Year's Eve, and she was so excited to finally have a father—someone who not only would cover her spiritually but now physically would be there to guide her as a father could and give the stability in their new home that Kamal was having built for the three of them once they married.

Tania's godparents and Aunt Shelby were all in on the surprise as well. Aunt Shelby's plane was to arrive early on New Year's Eve, and she'd stay the night with Ondrea and Tania and come to the service with them later that evening.

Both Bria and Tania went with Kamal to pick out her mother's ring from Tiffany & Co. They settled for the 2.02 Carat, Soleste Heart-shaped Halo ring with the Diamond Platinum Band. *$81,000 for a ring? He's crazy,* Tania thought to herself.

"That's what I'm talking about, brother-to-be!" Bria exclaimed. She was uber excited that her best friend was getting married again—this time to one of her husband's best friends, and more importantly—a Man of God. She had told Ondrea that she and Dearron were in town because their church was fellowshipping with Kamal's for Watch Night service, and she bought it.

"Thanks, sis," Kamal said with confidence. He wanted to make sure that everything was perfect—down to the congregation making sure that no one knew of his plan for the evening. "So what time is everyone showing up tonight?"

Bria informed Kamal of them arriving an hour before to make sure that they were in place as well as help ensure his plan is carried out effectively, while Tania told him that she was riding with her mother and Aunt Shelby.

*****

Kamal was so excited about tonight. Over the last couple of months, it had been so hard to keep his composure around her. They talked and Face timed every day and went on dates during the day in public places like the library, restaurants, and museums—even the amusement park—if they were in public, they were cool. He'd hoped that if she said yes, they could plan a wedding six months to a year away from the date. He wanted to also make sure that they were in order and went through the proper marriage counseling that their Senior Pastor offered. He looked in the mirror: *Here it goes, Lord...never thought I'd ever get to this space, but You did it for me, and suddenly. I thank and praise You for giving me such a precious gift...a family of my own. In Jesus' name, Amen.* He fixed the collar on his black Ralph Lauren tailored suit with the gold-accented tie, *It's showtime.*

*****

Ondrea was so excited that Aunt Shelby was in town and staying the night on top of attending Watch Night service with her and Tania. The only other time that her Aunt had come to visit her church, was when she got baptized. She just knew tonight was going to be special...to bring in the new year with her mother-figure, daughter, best friend, and her hubby—all while her "boo" was preaching the year in? *What could get any better than that?* She said to herself with so much gladness.

117

Kamal had asked her to match him with wearing black and gold. Ondrea stood there in a black and gold Dolce & Gabanna dress in matching heels and accessories, with her hair hanging down alongside her face in deep waves. She couldn't help but smile at the results when she took a glimpse of herself in the mirror.

"Come on Auntie and Tania!" she called out to them as she started towards the car.

Chapter Twenty-One

Mother Helen was seated on the second row and motioned for Ondrea and her family to sit next to her. Ondrea introduced her Aunt Shelby to Ms. Helen, and while they were getting acquainted with each other before the service started, Ondrea spotted Bria sitting on the first row, and they both exchanged smiles and waves before Dearron, and Kamal entered the sanctuary. All eyes and attention were on the two as they tag-teamed in leading the service. Finally, it was 11:43 pm, and Kamal was the final preacher to close out the service at midnight.

Ondrea could not wait to hear from her man. She loved watching him deliver the Word with such power and demonstration during Sunday services and Bible Study nights. As he looked at him while he started to deliver his "seventeen-minute message" as he always referred to his quicker sermons, she could not help but be proud of his strength during their dating and courting period. She thought about how well Tania and Kamal got along together, and how he already stepped up to fulfill some of the "fatherly duties" of teaching and instructing her, in addition to becoming a permanent fixture on family outings around the city and state. *God, You have really and truly blessed me.* Ondrea thought to herself.

"...So, as I close out...remember congregation that while God is the same yesterday, today, and forevermore, the constant remains in Him that He does a new thing when He desires, and all according to His timing...a time to find a loved one and hug, kiss...rejoice and praise Him for keeping You and them and bringing us into another new year!"

While Bria ran up to the pulpit to greet Dearron with a hug and kiss, Ondrea noticed Kamal coming down from the pulpit and meeting her in the aisle. She embraced him tightly.

"Happy New Year, babe!" she exclaimed.

"I want to kiss you so bad right now, in front of all these people." Kamal's stare into Ondrea's eyes was so intense, that she had to look away.

"Babe, people are looking at you crazy, plus you can't kiss me remember—you said when I'm your Mrs…"

Kamal dropped down on one knee and pulled out the infamous blue box. Everyone in the congregation gasped when he opened the box to display the ring. "I know lady, and I want to make that happen as soon as you say 'yes'…so will you have me as your husband, your protector, your lover, and life companion?"

Ondrea was shocked and ecstatic at the same time. She looked at Kamal, who was eagerly awaiting an answer. "Yes, yes, I will marry you, Kamal!"

Kamal got up off from the floor and swept Ondrea up into his arms kissing her on her forehead in such a loving and endearing way, and then pulling her close again for an embrace. "Thank you, baby," he added. "I love you so much Ondrea, and I can't wait to show you everything that I'm about," he said in her ear for only her to hear.

"I love you too, Kamal…I can't wait to give you all of me either. I look forward to the future God has for us."

The congregation erupted in cheers and whistles of happiness and approval of the new First-Lady-to-be in their ministry. Mother Helen and Aunt Shelby were both crying, while Tania and Londyn were jumping up and down with excitement.

When Ondrea returned home and said goodnight to Tania and Aunt Shelby, she laid down on her bed trying to process everything that had occurred. 2:44 AM…She dialed Kamal's number.

"Hey babe, he answered. "How are you feeling? I thought I wouldn't talk to you again until later today," he joked.

"I know, right…so, are we really getting married, Kamal?"

"I'm not playing no games with you, lady…wait a minute, are you starting to have second thoughts?"

"No, I'm just having a hard time processing all of this…I mean, the fact that not only am I going to be your wife, but the wife of a Pastor on top of it all…"

"Your girl Bria got you though. She can help you navigate through it all…Mother Helen also is ride or die, so you know," he joked again.

"I guess you're right…so when were you thinking of us doing this?"

"Well, I was hoping by Thanksgiving, I can add to my prayer that I am thankful for my new bride."

"A Thanksgiving wedding? I like that. It's intimate and centered around family…oh, Kamal you are someone special."

"Well, I try…anything for my lady. Now, you know we must complete marriage counseling…I think that'll be good for us. I want us to go into this marriage doing everything in order, and the right way."

"I'm with whatever you want babe. I am humbly following your lead, sir."

"I'm loving your approach to this already."

As Ondrea hung up the phone with her fiancé', she still felt as if she was in a dream. She would be the wife of a Preacher who was soon to become Pastor of the church. *Wow, life does surely change upon us when we least expect it.* She had a wedding to plan. Not going to the Justice of Peace as she did in her previous marriage to Chance, but an actual ceremony…*this experience will be different, for the better.*

Chapter Twenty-Two

Tania was so excited…Her birthday weekend was finally here. Friday would kick off the weekend with her and Londyn getting spa treatments at Buckhead Grand Spa (courtesy of Ms. Gewn), followed by her mother and Kamal's engagement party, then leading into her epic birthday party that night at the Cascade. She laid out her outfit for both the engagement party and her birthday: A black tutu dress from Forever 21 for the engagement party, and a Burberry flannel t-shirt dress with matching fishnet stockings. She had her red accessories and matching Burberry sneakers to match both outfits. She only hoped Londyn would do like she asked and match her colors on tonight for the pictures.

"Happy birthday, Valentine's baby!" exclaimed Londyn while she rushed to hug her best friend. She too was now a part of the "Sweet Sixteen" club, and now all they could think about was taking driver's ed classes so they could prepare to drive.

"Thanks so much, Londy!" squealed Tania. The two had settled for the half-day package just to take time to rest up for the events that were to follow.

"So, Miss-Missy…what's up with you and Sebastian? He's still on you, you know?"

"I know, but I'm not ready to give up my virginity…at least I don't feel the need to make sure that he has it. If he waits for me, cool and if not…then as much as it hurts, I have to keep it moving."

"Girl, I just knew ya'll were doing it the night at homecoming…all this time has passed, how come you didn't tell me what went down?"

"I don't know, I just kept it to myself…clearly you and my cousin were having such a great time up in his room. I didn't want to kill your excitement."

"Girl, I wish we hadn't been doing it so much…" she stated as she looked down at her belly.

"Swear?!" Tania gasped in shock at the sight of a small baby bump under Londyn's robe.

"I wish I could be joking with you…I still haven't told him, or anyone yet…I think that I am about three or four months now. I've been having my period so that's why I didn't think anything was wrong until I started throwing up more recently in the past two weeks."

"Well, I'm glad you shared your secret with me. You better keep the baby, and I can help tell my cousin. I think he'll be happy…it's his dad I'd be worried about…wait, your mom and dad?"

"I've just been in my room and keep wearing these sweatsuits for now. I dunno, Tania…I don't know if I can keep it any longer. I know I have to do something."

"Please don't, sissy. My godmother almost couldn't get pregnant—let alone stay pregnant enough to have her son because she had abortions before."

"I know all of the risks; I just don't want my life changed forever."

"I hear you, but in the meantime, that baby is growing until you do something...I'll love you regardless."

"Thanks so much, Tania. I needed to hear that."

"But I would love to be an auntie to a niece or a nephew…. T is serious about you, though. If you guys make it to eighteen, you two could get married…you'd be my family for real…"

"I'm thinking still, Tania…"

"Well, I need an answer soon, Mamas," Tania said as she playfully nudged her.

Chapter Twenty-Three

Ondrea and Kamal made the final arrangements for Tania's surprise car that was to arrive at the finale of her birthday party at Cascade: An S 560 Mercedes-Benz coupe. They went in half to purchase the car, with Kamal stating that he would keep up the maintenance and insurance payments on it. He did alright as the Associate Pastor, but once they married on Thanksgiving, he would also be made the Senior Pastor and presider over the church and its congregation—also increasing his finances.

The place was decorated in red and black so elegantly (the theme for Tania's birthday). The savory smells of good food from Que Jays Catering coming from the kitchen/dining area. The red and black customized sweet treats provided by Sugar Kouture and Premium By the Pound were sure to be a hit as well. DJ J. Hearns, one of the dopest female DJs in the US flew in to spin some of the greatest R&B and Soul songs for the occasion.

Both Kamal and Ondrea made sure that they were dressed in black and red. They decided to keep the engagement dinner as intimate as possible. They had only invited: Mother Helen, Dearron and Bria, Taylor (she left her husband and filed for divorce), T and Tyrin, along with Marie and Sienna. Aunt Shelby couldn't get a flight back in time to join in the festivities, but she was there in spirit. Tania and Londyn both were set to attend some of the party, but then they, along with T would be heading over to Cascade to kick off Tania's birthday party there where the rink was rented out for the entire freshman class, with a few sophomore exceptions—T being one of them.

Everyone arrived looking classy and dapper—even Tyrin had cleaned up nice in an Armani suit.

Kamal tapped his glass with a knife to get everyone's attention. "Before Tania and 'the Crew' run off, I'd like to make sure that we sing 'Happy Birthday' to her…I thank God for you, and you accepting me in your family, and allowing me to be somewhat of a father figure for you. I won't take that role for granted that I am charged with walking in, and only pray that I do not fail you or your mother in my role as the head of our family."

As everyone 'oohed' and 'aahed' at Kamal's words, and finished singing "Happy Birthday," Tania rushed towards Kamal to hug him, he could feel the cold stare coming from Tyrin. *Dude better not cause any drama at our celebration. Lord, please help keep me and my temper from raging. Allow peace to prevail during our time of celebration. In Jesus' name, Amen.*

"Thanks so much, Minister Kamal…I love you so much for my mom. She's been through so much, and I'm thankful that God put you two together," she said as Kamal hugged her back, with Ondrea smiling with tears in her eyes.

Although Ondrea was happy that she was marrying the newfound love of her life, she couldn't help but catch a glimpse of the look on Tyrin's face, which brought her back to the realization that the chapter of the life with Chance and everything tied to it had served its purpose, and now it was time to move forward.

*****

Kamal raised a champagne flute filled with sparkling grape juice. "I'd like to start with a toast to the two men who have been in Ondrea and Tania's life before I came in the picture…Tyrin and Dearron. Tyrin: I can only imagine how hard it must've been for you to step into such a major role while grieving the loss of their head of the family and your blood. Much respect to you, and I pray that I make you proud also."

126

Tyrin nodded his head in agreement simply mumbled, "thanks."

Kamal continued in the next toast to Dearron. "My boy, I thank you for also standing in the gap in making sure my bonus daughter and my lady were straight—most importantly, thank you for inviting me back to your crib after that service where I met Ondrea. It's been nothing short of amazing ever since for the both of us, and I cannot thank you enough, bro…Salute," as he raised his champagne flute.

"Salute," D replied. "I knew you two would be a perfect match."

"Now to the women in Ondrea's life: 'Bri-Bri,' thank you for approving of me hooking up with your girl…going with me and Tania to help set up everything perfect for my proposal…Taylor and Marie, thank you, ladies, for also accepting me…my prayer also is that I do not let you guys down. I will do my best with everything in me and the direction from God to take care of, love, and respect your girl…. Salute," he raised his glass.

"We love you, man!" Bria said excitedly, raising her glass to Kamal.

Kamal turned towards Ondrea, "Do you want to make any toasts, lady?"

"Yeah," she said full of emotion and trying to hold back tears. "I'm gonna get through this…Tyrin, what can I say? You have been a constant in both Tania and I's life. I hope you know that in this next chapter of our lives you still have a place as family…once family, always family," she stammered through her tears as she raised her glass to Tyrin.

Tyrin raised his glass out of respect to Ondrea and shed one tear, and then got up to excuse himself to the restroom. Taylor got up from the table to run off after him.

Bria watched in awe at the sight of Taylor running to his rescue. Although she was happily married to Dearron, her heart longed to be with Tyrin. When Bria was sixteen, Tyrin helped stop a man from brutally raping her one night while her pimp had her turning tricks. Tyrin and his crew took care of her pimp, and from that day Bria was free from the chains of sex trafficking. Since then, Bria held Tyrin in the place of her 'hero' and protector. Though they only messed around once, that night they exchanged some serious familiar spirits of brokenness and pain that created a huge soul tie.

Over the years up until he went to jail, Bria and Tyrin would continue to mess around. After he went to jail, she swore she would never cheat on Dearron again. One drunk night, Tyrin had played a song for her by Tank entitled, "You Never Knew," when he dialed her cell phone and reached her voicemail. That song described how the woman never knew the whole time he had interacted with her that he wanted to "wife her." She knew that she would never leave Dearron no matter what because this life was what was good for her, and what God desired for her.

The fact that Taylor and Tyrin appeared to be involved with each other infuriated her, but she knew she had no right to be upset while she was indeed a married woman, and happy that Taylor could finally pursue true happiness with someone who would be as into her as she was them. As she collected her thoughts and tried to make sure her thoughts weren't written across her face, she noticed D's look of puzzlement as to what was bothering his wife about what just happened with Tyrin.

Ondrea putting two and two together quickly intervened with another toast. "D and Bria…what can I say? The power couple, who has it all…I thank you for pushing me to have my happily ever after like you guys. Thank you for introducing me to this fine man, here!" she exclaimed raising her glass in a toast. Both raised theirs in solidarity.

"Mother Helen," she continued. "Thanks so much for welcoming me into your church and taking me under your wing during our courtship. You have become like family to me, and I thank God for you," she raised her glass and Mother Helen joined her.

"Marie…I love you," Ondrea raised her glass again with Marie and Sienna joining her. "Alright now everyone, let's get our groove on before it's time to surprise Tania at Cascade."

All the jams were played…from "I Want You Around" by Snoah Aalegra, to "Alone Together" by Daley feat. Marsha Ambrosius, to "You and I" by Avant and KeKe Wyatt, and "Be Close to You," by BeBe & CeCe Winans. Tyrin and Taylor came back from the restroom letting everyone know it was getting close to ten o'clock, so they all needed to head to the skating rink.

*****

Once they all arrived out front of Cascade, you could hear the hits banging as DJ Killa Kev was always in the building on Friday nights. Tyrin parked Tania's gift right at the front door and got out to join everyone else in the group. Kamal stated that he would go inside to pay for any final charges the kids had racked up. As a truce to their obvious tensions and indifferences unbeknownst to both, Tyrin offered to pay for half.

"Thanks, bro…I appreciate you even if you don't think so."

"It's cool, I just had to feel you out first… 'Drea is more like a little sis to me, so I take the affairs of her heart personal."

"I feel you," Kamal stated matter-of-factly.

"Alright, 'Ice'…thanks again for your business," the man at the counter stated.

"I told you, I'm not in the life anymore, bro," Kamal said sternly to the man. "I'd appreciate it if you don't call me by that name anymore."

Tyrin stopped walking dead in his tracks and turned around. "What you call him?"

It was at that moment, Kamal recognized who Tyrin was, and he also the same.

"Hey Tyrin and Minister Kamal, what are ya'll talking about?" Tania asked as she realized something was up.

"None of your business, birthday brat...now let's all go on outside to the afterparty…"

"Oooh! Thanks, Tyrin!" she squealed as Tania, T, Londyn, and the rest of the students who were left all headed towards her surprise.

"This ain't over nigga," Tyrin gritted through his teeth with clenched fists. It was taking everything in him not to beat Kamal down right then and there.

After Tania, T, and her friends drove off in her new Mercedes, Tyrin then stepped up in Kamal's face.

"Preacher-boy, tell me you not who I think you are… DON'T LIE, NIGGA!" Tyrin then shouted while he started shaking beyond control with rage.

"I can explain…" Kamal started to reply.

Ondrea ran up to the two of them to see why Tyrin was so visibly upset and causing commotion. "What is going on?!" she demanded, scared and anxious seeing the two of them glaring at one another.

"Tell her, nigga…tell her what the problem is, 'Ice'!"

"'Ice?' I-I don't understand, Kamal…Tyrin…what's going on?"

130

"This is the nigga whose boy killed Chance!"

Ondrea felt numb. She felt her heart beating faster and faster by the second, and her head started to spin. "I-Is this true, Kamal?"

Kamal lowered his head in shame. He couldn't face the woman of his dreams enough to look her in the eye to admit that he was the reason her heart broke for the first time. "I-I'm so sorry, baby…I didn't know…I…" before he could finish his statement, Tyrin cold-cocked his fist back and punched Kamal in the mouth with all his might. Ondrea passed out.

~To Be Continued~

Join Love Series Email List at: <u>Beautyfromashesllc44@gmail.com</u>

<u>Follow for updates!!!!!</u>

FB: @theloveseries44

IG: authorcarriefarley

<u>Previous Books:</u>

Love Chances